HELL'S VENGEANCE

HELL'S VENGEANCE SERIES BOOK 2

IAN FORTEY

AND

RON RIPLEY

EDITED BY MICHELLE BROWNE
AND ANNE LAO

ISBN: 9798398049527
Copyright © 2023 by ScareStreet.com

THANK YOU AND BONUS NOVEL!

We'd like to take a moment to thank you for your ongoing support. You make this all possible! To really show you our appreciation for purchasing this book, **we'd love to send you a full-length horror novel in 3 formats (MOBI, EPUB and PDF) absolutely free!**

Download your full-length horror novel, get free short stories, and receive future discounts by visiting www.ScareStreet.com

See you in the shadows,
Team Scare Street

PROLOGUE

Detroit never truly went to sleep. *God, but it should*, Benny Aubrey thought. The sound was just always there. It was a droning kind of hum, the machine of the whole city at work. Not the sound of life, that was too generous. It was more an endless death rattle.

He really hated being in Detroit. Hated the smell of it, hated the look of it, hated the people—everything. But he wasn't leaving. He couldn't. Not any time soon.

He was a resident of the Wayne County Community Correctional Center, a for-profit halfway house run by a Florida-based company, in conjunction with the Michigan Department of Corrections. As part of his early-release agreement, Benny was obliged to stay within county limits at all times. Once the sun went down, he had to be on halfway house grounds, or face being shipped back to prison.

He could have been serving his full sentence on a cell block again, but he'd lucked into the program—and to be fair, earned it as well. He'd been trying to fly on the straight and narrow for a few years now. He was getting too old to get jammed up in stupid crap. He had a family out there, a kid he'd only met once and a woman who could have been his wife. She hadn't returned his calls in a long time. But there was always hope for tomorrow. That's what all the counselors kept saying. That and other self-affirmational garbage.

Truth be told, Benny was just tired of the hustle. Of the friends he had when he was a kid, more were now dead than alive. And for what? Not one of them ever hit it big. None of them lived the dream, or even got within reach of it. They'd just heaped stupid on stupid and had nothing to show for it. He hated it. He despised himself for being a part of it. But now all that was left was to turn around and head back to something—anything—else.

Problem was, as far as Benny could see, when a man got to a certain age and had enough on his record, then all the regret and good intentions in the world didn't amount to anything. How did you go straight when that world didn't want you?

Benny's plan was not so much to go straight as to maybe go a little less crooked. On a slant. He wasn't going to be doing anything too dangerous or too stupid, but facts were facts, and bills needed to get paid. And that was how he found himself in the backyard of the W4C after curfew, making a deal with a guy named Hambone through a hole in the fence.

Benny still had connections and could still move product. Not a lot, but enough to get by. People owed him favors, so they were willing to let him take a more relaxed approach to selling, especially given his situation. Dealing out of a halfway house had risks. Too many, in fact. But he kept it low-key, and never sold to other residents.

If he was going to straighten up and fly right or whatever other things the counselors liked to say, he needed a base. He needed seed money, something real. Not a part-time minimum wage job, where the boss could treat him like crap because he knew Benny was a felon and wouldn't complain. That was how things worked. Maybe one in ten businesses that signed up for the program were those unicorn gigs run by a Mother Teresa who sincerely believed in second chances. The rest were people who could make you work unpaid hours, or file paperwork saying you got paid more than you did, so they could skim off the top. And they got away with it because no one checked. No one cared.

Hambone had been a good customer because he rarely spoke, never stood out, and was always on time. One of those punctual guys. Who would have guessed?

The yard behind W4C was a chunk of enclosed green space meant to be a relaxation or meditation spot for the facility's residents. In the daylight, some guys would read back there, and if you tried hard, you could maybe have half a football game. It wasn't a big yard, but it wasn't small either.

The fence line had been landscaped with medium-sized fir trees, and they made decent enough cover. Hambone passed the cash through; Benny passed a small bag. To anyone who might have been watching, it looked like he was just really into touching trees in the dark.

If he got caught in the yard, he'd get a write up and probably get toilet-cleaning duty for a week. "No yard after dark" was a hard and fast rule. W4C worked on an honor system for a lot of stuff. If you hung yourself by your own actions for enough screw-ups, they'd send you back to lock up.

Most guys followed the rules really well. The house was basically a reward. You got freedom, better food, more privacy, and more time outdoors. You could get a job, go out during the day, and be in the world, like a real person again. Most guys were smart enough to not ruin it for themselves. Didn't hurt that so long as you attended regular counseling and behaved well in the house, it knocked time off your sentence, too.

Hambone grunted a quiet thanks. Benny heard him shuffle down the road, then waited a moment before heading back to the house. He should have been inside about an hour earlier, but hopefully no one would notice. In the evening, most guys were either working out, watching TV, or reading. Night staff were kind of lazy and didn't pay a lot of attention to who was doing what and where. They'd do a ten o'clock bed check, and that was about it.

From the small cement patio that led into the rear hallway of the house, he approached the door. Then he heard a voice. "Benjamin, what are the rules about the garden at night?"

Benny gritted his teeth and held in a curse.

To him, Jocelyn Price's voice was like nails on a chalkboard. Not that it was shrill, necessarily; he just hated having her around. The woman was one of a trio of counselors that worked in the house, and it seemed like she was always there. She was supposed to work normal hours, but it seemed like no one had told her that.

"Mrs. Price," Benny said as the elderly woman stood in the doorway and blocking his path. She looked like a sick bird that had lost all of its feathers—just loose pink skin over awkward shapes. She was a frail old woman, and he could have probably lifted her up with one hand and thrown her over the fence.

"Benjamin, we've been over this. The rules have to be followed. It's for your own good as much as anyone's. Following the rules shows you're trying. Shows you want to be good. Don't you want to be good?"

Her voice was equal parts sweet and fake. Most other guys seemed to like her because she could be cool sometimes. She'd brought in *Die Hard* for a movie night once, even though the rules said you weren't supposed to watch violent stuff. She would order pizza once a month, too. But something about her still rubbed him the wrong way.

"You know me, Mrs. Price. I'm good as gold," he joked.

She offered him a tight-lipped smile. "You've been making progress, Benjamin. How much longer until your release?"

"Eight months," he told her. He wouldn't call anything he'd done "progress", but he was flying under the radar and doing what he needed to do. Maybe that was all it took.

"Eight months. Be a shame to jeopardize that with something as silly as spending time outside after dark. What are you even doing out here?"

Benny let his eyes dart around. It didn't look like anyone else was around. No one that he could see had ratted him out. She must have just stumbled on him by accident. Three hours after her shift ended, but still by accident.

"Just needed some air. It's nice out here after dark. I didn't think it'd matter too much since I wasn't doing anything bad. I was just enjoying the peace and quiet."

"But it does matter, Benjamin. Just like it mattered the last time you were caught back here. Or did you forget?" she asked.

"No. No, ma'am, I did not forget," he said, shaking his head.

"Did I ever tell you that I used to have a substance abuse problem?" she asked suddenly.

Benny suppressed a sigh. She had told everyone this. Many, many times. It was a main feature of her drug counseling group sessions. She used to abuse painkillers and hid her addiction for years until she lost her family and ended up in the hospital but she decided to turn her life around and blah blah blah…

"You have. And I get it, Mrs. Price. I do. But I'm not using, you can get me a UA right now, if you don't believe me."

"No," Price agreed, looking him up and down for a moment. "You were never a user though, were you? You sold it. You went to prison for dealing," she said, snickering slightly.

Benny nodded. "But I'm turning my life around. Just like you did all those years ago."

She smiled. "Just like I did. New lease on life."

"Exactly."

"In each of us is the capacity to do good and evil, Benjamin. It's all about choices, isn't it?"

"I'll agree to that."

She then stepped back and held the door open for him. "Come inside. We can talk more at our next appointment."

He paused, cautiously optimistic. "Am I getting a write-up for this?"

"Do you want me to write you up for this?" she countered.

"No," he said bluntly.

5

She nodded. "Then no. But it won't happen again, will it?"

"No ma'am," he promised as he entered the house.

"Walk me to my office," she said, as he started on his way up to his room.

He suppressed another curse then turned. "Sure."

The rear hallway led to a stairwell, which they took up together. Price's office was on the third floor. He pushed open the door leading to the administrative offices and let her pass before following her.

The administrative office area of the halfway house always smelled weirdly antiseptic and was the only carpeted part of the building. Their footsteps were silenced on the ugly short-pile carpet that looked like purple and blue vomit. She talked about inane and unimportant things, and Benny nodded when it was appropriate.

She led the way down the hall, along the bank of windows that looked out over the front of the property and into the park beyond. At night, there was little to see past the streetlights, but the loud, ugly sounds of the city still filtered in. Car horns and engines and the occasional shout from some random drunk.

At the end of the hall, a dark wooden door was labeled with the number 7. Below that, on a tiny golden plaque with black letters, was a name that read "J. Price".

"Thank you, Benjamin. I'll see you soon," she stated.

Benny nodded again. "You have a good night, Mrs. Price."

He turned away before she could start talking again. Luckily, she did not. Instead, she slipped into her office and closed the door behind her.

Benny was only a few steps down the hall when he heard a loud thump from Price's office.

He paused, listening for any movement, but there was nothing. "Mrs. Price?" he asked, turning back to the door. Still no answer.

Benny approached and knocked, leaning his head close to listen in. "Mrs. Price, are you okay?"

Silence was his only reply. He reached for the doorknob and turned it slowly. Entering a staff office without permission was also a violation, but this had to be okay.

"Mrs. Price, I'm coming in," he stated loudly, pushing the door open.

The office was as neat and tidy as ever, with the exception of the elderly woman passed out on the floor in the center of the room. This time, Benny did curse out loud. Part of him was concerned for her well-being, but part of him was afraid he'd somehow get the blame for whatever happened.

He came to her side and knelt, putting a hand on her shoulder, and giving her a light shake.

"Mrs. Price!" he said loudly, but there was still no response. If she was dead, then he'd have hell of a time explaining himself. Not in his room after curfew, and at her office after hours. None of it looked good.

He needed to check her pulse. That was the first step. He reached out, touching the papery flesh of her neck. His hand grew cold. Terribly cold, almost painfully so. And then his vision clouded over black.

✳

Benjamin Aubrey stood—unsurely at first, wobbling as though drunk. It took only a moment for him to get his bearings. He turned away from the body on the floor and walked back the way he had come.

He went up the stairs, passed the fourth floor and continued up to the roof. Residents did some gardening on the rooftop, but nighttime access was, as with everything else, restricted. Not that it mattered just then.

With no hesitation, Benjamin walked to the edge of the roof on the east side of the building, just above the wrought iron fence that wrapped around the property, and jumped off.

He made no sound as he fell. No sound as the ornate fleur-de-lis fence post toppers pushed through his flesh, then right back out of his body again. And still no sound as he died.

Just then, Jocelyn Price stirred on the floor at her office. She got to her feet and headed to the window. She saw Benjamin Aubrey's impaled body several feet below her, a pool of his blood still quite visible in the darkness. He reminded her of skewered meat at a barbecue, and it made her smile.

She closed her curtains and sat down at her desk.

CHAPTER 1
BLOODLETTING

"I think this place is cursed," Detective Denise Sandoval said, turning the wheel of the car and slowing down onto the side street next to the Wayne County Community Correctional Center. It was the third time she and her partner Detective Jacinta Perez had caught wind of a suicide at the halfway house.

"Maybe they just feed everyone Nutraloaf," Jacinta suggested. At a lot of prisons, the almost-but-not-quite-food product was served to inmates—typically as a punishment. It was technically edible and nutritionally complete, ground up from whatever was on hand and baked as a loaf. She'd tried it once, and never wanted to see it again.

"Yeah, I can see that pushing guys over the edge," Sandoval said with the hint of a smile. She was not exactly in the mood for cracking jokes due to the rising number of suicide cases at the facility, but she had to admit it was a good one.

The last two cases at the halfway house had only barely come across Jacinta's desk. She worked homicide, and these were suicides, which had seemed pretty cut and dry at the time. A halfway house was always steeped in desperation, and the victims were men who'd been having harder times than most. But this latest case was something else.

Benjamin Aubrey, better known as Benny, had been a low-level dealer. Benny had an unusual ability to charm people and weasel his way into more places than a cockroach. He had his fingers in a dozen much bigger pies and knew most of the major players in the game. And that got the attention of the police.

Benny had been privy to information about several unsolved gang murders, so a friend in Vice got ahold of Jacinta and put Benny on her radar. The two had than met, talked, and worked out a deal. For years, Benny had been feeding Jacinta tips on unsolved murders, with a few having been directly linked to arrests and prosecutions.

In exchange, Benny had managed to all but get himself out of his former life. It took a few strategic arrests and some mandatory jail time, along with the sense that he had not, in fact, rolled on anyone. That all made sure Benny looked like a solid guy to his old crew, while also ensuring he had an escape plan. All he had to do was serve his time, most of it in a halfway house, and he'd be all but a free man.

Jacinta knew Benny was not suicidal.

If it had been anyone else who had died, she might have never even glanced at the file again. Halfway house suicides didn't get investigated a lot. The justice system was not overly invested in caring about something that looked open and shut.

And if Jacinta didn't know the man as well as she did, Benny would have slipped through the cracks, too.

They called the place the W4C for short, since the name was so ponderous. It looked and sounded official, but it was a for-profit facility run by a private company contracted out by the state. The rules in place were not laws. The whole thing seemed sketchy to Jacinta. She didn't like for-profit facilities. They had too much incentive to do things the wrong way.

Benny had been discovered by one of the facility guards before sunrise. It was still early in the morning when Jacinta and Sandoval arrived, a tray of coffee in tow. Uniformed officers were keeping the area clear, although there were already a gaggle of residents with their faces pressed to the windows inside. They eagerly watched the medical examiner and the police working around the body speared on the fence.

"Mark," Sandoval said, nodding at the medical examiner. She handed the short man a cup of coffee and gave the fourth cup in the cardboard tray to a uniformed officer on the scene.

"Detectives," Mark Pavelski replied, nodding thanks for the coffee. "Victim was a thirty-six-year-old male. Apparent suicide. Cause of death—"

"Impaled on a fence," Sandoval finished the sentence before taking a sip of her coffee.

Mark nodded. "Apparently. Three posts pierced the body—one through the heart, which would have killed him instantly. We'll have to do a tox screen to determine if drugs were involved, of course. Time of death was sometime last night; I'd say before ten o'clock. The trees out front here, and the fact the facility doesn't allow people in and out after sundown, meant he was undiscovered until the morning shift."

"Does anything suggest not suicide?" Jacinta asked, looking at the body. Benny's eyes were open, staring down at nothing. She wasn't sure how Mark and his team would get the body off the fence without damaging it further. The fence post tops were barbed like arrowheads.

"No signs of any additional trauma to suggest a struggle. Angle of the body is consistent with someone who jumped. CSI would be checking the rooftop for evidence he was pushed, but just basing it off the body, it's looking pretty solid."

Jacinta nodded, drinking her own coffee. She looked at the ground, at the large pool of blood. The edges had dried dark, but the center was thick and congealed. Insects were already clustered at the edges to have a taste.

"You knew him better than I did," Sandoval stated.

"Yeah. He was a schemer. Crafty guy. Horseshoes up his ass, too. He'd been planning his transition back to a normal life for years."

"Maybe something went sour."

"Maybe," Jacinta agreed. She knew he had a kid out there, and an ex who wanted nothing to do with him. Didn't seem like it could get worse than that.

"Not feeling it?" Sandoval said then.

"No."

"Well then. Detective work it is."

She turned away from the body and walked toward the main entrance to the facility. A thin man in a drab gray suit waited by the door, looking extremely uncomfortable.

"Hi, my name is Dana Sherman. I'm the administrator of W Four C. If there's anything I can do to help speed this along, Officers, please—"

"Detectives," Sandoval interrupted.

Sherman paused. He had a strangely long face and looked to be in his early fifties. His skin had a rumpled appearance, like the dewlaps of a bloodhound. "I'm sorry?"

"You said 'officers', Mr. Sherman. We're detectives. What can you tell us about the deceased?"

"Yes. Detectives." He looked unimpressed. "His name was Benjamin Aubrey. I have his file for you. He was incarcerated with distribution of illegal substances. Um, narcotics. Selling narcotics. But a reduced sentence for cooperating on some case or other."

"Some case or other?" Jacinta asked.

Sherman spread his hands out apologetically. "You'll have to forgive me. I've only been the administrator here for a week. The previous administrator was recently let go, and I'm just catching up with the general day-to-day. I haven't had much of a chance to get to know the individual residents very well just yet."

"Who *does* know the individual residents well?" Sandoval asked.

"I believe Jocelyn Price would have the most information for you. She's one of our counselors and has done the most one-on-one work with Mr. Aubrey. She does group and individual counseling sessions, and really strives to develop a personal connection with all of our residents."

"Is she here now?" Sandoval inquired.

Sherman nodded. "Yes, of course. This way, please."

He led them into the facility, which reminded Jacinta of a strange cross between a hospital and a high school. It was the design aesthetic—plain hallways, drab paint, and a pair of cameras pointed right at the entrance—and even the smell. A man in khakis and a polo shirt, who must have been a guard of some sort, sat at a desk with a sign-in book.

"Please," Sherman said, gesturing to the book. Sandoval signed in first, followed by Jacinta.

"Do we have footage of Aubrey on the roof?" Jacinta asked, gesturing to the cameras.

"I'm afraid not," Sherman replied, leading them down a hall. "Our cameras only monitor the exits. This is not a prison, so we don't surveil our residents at all times."

"Three apparent suicides in such a short span of time, though? Maybe you should," Sandoval suggested.

Sherman glanced at her. "I can't imagine how cameras would have made a difference."

Sandoval glanced at Jacinta but said nothing. Jacinta rolled her eyes. Sherman needed to work on his people skills. Or at least his Sandoval skills.

They made their way to a stairwell, then headed up to the third floor. They passed a number of other men dressed like the man at the door, indicating that khaki pants and polo shirts were, in fact, some sort of official guard uniform at the facility.

"Any guards on duty last night?" Jacinta asked.

"We have *monitors* here, not guards. And we did have monitors on duty, but they are reduced after hours. No one saw anything."

"So, you asked?"

"Of course, I asked," Sherman replied.

"We'd like to talk to those *monitors*." Sandoval mirrored the man's emphasis on the word.

"I assure you—"

"If you can have them ready to talk to us after we're done speaking to Aubrey's counselor, that would be very helpful," Sandoval interrupted him once more. She nodded to a door down the hall with the plaque that read "J. Price". "We're good from here. If we have any additional questions, we'll find you."

"Visitors aren't permitted to be unescorted within the facility, I'm afraid."

"Visitors," Sandoval said with a smile. "Alright. Well, I'm sure you can find someone to show us around. We don't want to take up any more of your time. Thank you, Mr. Sherman."

She stood her ground, waiting for Sherman to leave, while Jacinta looked out the nearest window. Below them, she could see that Aubrey's body had been removed from the fence and was now in a body bag on the pavement.

"I will have one of my men come to escort you shortly," Sherman replied before leaving.

Sandoval joined Jacinta at the window and looked down. "Hell of a way to go, huh?"

Jacinta nodded. "Too early in the morning for you to be making friends," she said as the door loudly closed behind Sherman.

Her partner shrugged. "Let's talk to Price. Maybe she's a little more helpful."

"Sure. Just give me a second. I need to make a call."

She headed down the hall away from Sandoval as she pulled out her phone. Nothing was standing out as overly suspicious yet, but at the same time, there was a feeling in her gut she couldn't ignore. She had pulled files on murders and suicides in the neighborhood before they'd arrived. There were too many, too close together.

And they all started at the end of Wyatt Hawthorn's reign of terror.

CHAPTER 2
BECKONING

There was a breeze blowing through the garden, and in most other places, it would have been a nice day. No birds sang in the trees here, of course, and despite the sunshine, there was a gray pallor over the yard. The air had a habitual chill around the house on Berkely Street.

Shane Ryan was seated on the steps, looking out at nothing in particular. A half-empty cup of tepid coffee sat next to him, and the cigarette between his fingers burned slowly.

"You are becoming pensive in your old age, my young friend," Carl said to him in German. The ghost sat next to him, his eyes directed out at the world as well.

Shane smiled slightly at the curious paradox in the ghost's phrasing. "Isn't this what people do? They sit and look at the world and think?"

"Do they? I only know you, and you rarely do this."

"Must have read it somewhere," Shane replied, taking a drag on the cigarette. Smoke swirled around him as he exhaled, and then vanished, his own tobacco-born spirit destroyed in moments.

"Spirits don't do it much either."

"Except you."

"In this instance, yes," Carl agreed. "Because I sense something different in you. You have been home, for too long."

"I went out for cigarettes yesterday," Shane countered.

"Being obtuse does not become you."

"I think I take to it well," Shane argued.

It was true, though. He had been home for quite some time now with little to do. The few people in his life that he considered friends had been busy of late. The problems that had a way of falling into his lap had not fallen for a while. It gave him more time to himself than usual. There was just not much going on in his world. He should have appreciated that. That was another thing normal people did. They enjoyed calm, non-dangerous lives.

He took another drag on his cigarette just as the phone in his pocket rang. He glanced at Carl who returned the look.

"Have we manifested something to occupy your time?" the spirit asked.

"We don't *manifest*." Shane rolled his eyes as he fished his phone out of his pocket.

"I believe I do." Carl shrugged.

Shane read Jacinta's name on his phone screen and pressed the answer button.

"Shane, how are you?" Jacinta said as he pressed the phone to his ear.

"Smoking," he replied.

She laughed. "Of course. Sorry for calling so early, but I've got something here that seems a little weird."

"Weird how?" The last time he had been with her on something weird, they were taking on the ghost of a serial killer.

"I'm working a suicide case at a halfway house. Thing is, I don't think it was a suicide."

"Okay."

"I knew the vic. Informant of mine. Not a model citizen, sure, but not the scum of the earth, either. Suicide was not in his character, though."

"Are you saying he was murdered?"

"Yeah, maybe. What's bothering me more is... well, there have been

17

a string of suicides in the area. A couple in the halfway house, and more in the immediate surroundings. Too many in such a short time. Things are starting to look off. And the halfway house is in a familiar location—it's right by the meatpacking plant."

Shane took another drag on his cigarette. "Hawthorn's meatpacking plant?"

"That's the one," she confirmed.

Wyatt Hawthorn had been a member of the Ontario Provincial Police in Canada. He'd also been a prolific serial killer for years. After being killed by the ghost of one of his victims, his spirit took over the body of a man named Chris Jessop. Jessop then headed to Detroit to continue his work, owing in part to an obsession he had developed with Jacinta. Shane had destroyed Hawthorn in the meatpacking plant, but that had been months ago. According to Jacinta, the plant had even been demolished, with a new structure being built in its place already close to completion. It had been that long ago. And with Hawthorn having been twice removed from the world of the living, there was no way he could return.

"You don't think it's Hawthorn, do you?" Shane asked.

"No, not him. But if I got a bunch of people offing themselves in the same place where a ghost had done horrible things, it's just making my alarms go off."

"Understandable," Shane agreed. If she hadn't known the victim, then maybe he'd be less inclined to think something was up. A ghost did have the ability to make a possessed person hurt themselves. But with Hawthorn gone, their list of suspects was at zero. "So, what are you thinking?"

"Maybe it has nothing to do with Hawthorn at all, but something here doesn't add up. And the timing is just too much of a coincidence. You'll never guess what I found when I looked into it."

"Surprise me."

"Gangbangers had been killed at the park near the meatpacking plant on the same day you destroyed Hawthorn. One of them killed his buddies, then took himself out. Happened just after we left the scene. It written up as a murder-suicide."

"There's a coincidence," he agreed.

"Yeah. A violent one, too. The others have been less gruesome, but all involved suicide. And they all seem to be people with criminal backgrounds. Isn't that weird?"

He took another puff on the cigarette, the ember burning down to the filter, and then exhaled as he stared out at his grim, silent yard.

"It is."

"So, what do you think?"

"I think I'll be seeing you soon."

They said their goodbyes, and he hung up the phone.

"Sounds like you have something to do at last," Carl told him in German.

Shane nodded, picking up his coffee and finishing it. It was cold at this point, but he didn't mind.

"Maybe," he replied. He didn't see all the dots Jacinta was connecting, but he trusted her instincts. She knew when something smelled off, and if this was off to her, it was worth looking into.

"Back to Detroit, then?" Carl asked.

"Looks like it."

He stood up, taking his coffee cup with him, and headed back into the house. He'd pack a few things and be on the road in no time. If he was quick, he could be in Detroit before sundown.

The others in the house, especially Eloise, would be annoyed that he'd be leaving again. She didn't like it when he left. But Shane had not seen Jacinta in some time though, and truth be told, he was glad for the opportunity.

Even if it came with the baggage of suicide at best and ghostly murders at worst.

CHAPTER 3
IN THE WEB

Sandoval knocked loudly on the door to Jocelyn Price's office.

"Jocelyn Price?" she said loudly.

"One moment," came a muffled reply from within. There was a quiet sound of shuffling, and then the door opened. A woman who looked like she did not belong in a residential facility full of felons opened the door and smiled broadly.

Jocelyn Price was at least five inches shorter than Sandoval, and her white hair was pulled back in a tight bun. She looked extremely frail, but her eyes were bright, her smile warm, and she had a curious vigor about the way she held herself.

"Oh, my. You must be with the police. Don't see a lot of women in here," Price said, grinning from ear to ear. She looked from Sandoval to Jacinta, and her smile brightened.

"Detectives Perez and Sandoval," Jacinta said. "We're here to ask you some questions about—"

"About Benjamin Aubrey, of course. Please, come in," she said, holding her door open.

Jacinta and Sandoval entered the small office, which was accented with wooden furniture, houseplants, and little knick-knacks on every shelf. There were books, a small sofa, and a pair of chairs in front of what looked like an antique desk.

The elderly woman gestured toward the chairs in front of her desk as she sat across from them.

"Mr. Sherman tells us you worked with Mr. Aubrey," Sandoval said.

Price nodded. "Yes, I'd spent a good deal of time with him as a counselor here. We spoke a few times per week."

"You were friendly, then?" Sandoval continued.

"As friendly as I am with everyone here."

"What kind of counseling do you do with the residents?"

"Oh," Price said, smiling and leaning back slightly in her chair. "You need to be a jack of all trades here. It can be career counseling one day, dealing with home and family another. Sometimes, it will be about transitional issues, even drug counseling."

"What was the nature of your work with Mr. Aubrey?"

"We had a group counseling session twice per week, focused on career and transition. Dealing with 'getting back to the real world,' as they say. And we would also talk one-on-one about his plans for the future, his past; whatever he felt like, really. Such a shame what happened to him."

"Did he ever give you the impression he was suicidal?" Jacinta asked.

Price smiled at her, then sighed. "Recently, he had been having a tough time with things. He had a growing anxiety over his return to society, a fear that he wouldn't be able to adapt and straighten his life out as he'd wanted. I had been trying to encourage him, but it was clearly worse than I realized."

"Had there been any indication of depression?" Jacinta asked.

"Well, I'm not a clinician, but yes, I feel that's accurate. I thought maybe I could help keep him focused, but I caught him dealing drugs last night, and I knew things were getting bad. But he promised the two of us could talk today, and I thought we'd have time to work on it."

"What kind of drugs?" Sandoval asked.

"Oh, I can't be sure, but it was clearly something."

"Did you report him?" Jacinta inquired.

The elderly woman's smile was as bright as ever and was becoming oddly unnerving. "I haven't. Because I believe in second chances. That's why I work here, after all. I wanted to believe I could get through to Benjamin."

"You let a convicted drug dealer off the hook for drug possession inside a halfway house?" Sandoval was unable to hide her confusion.

"I know—it sounds awful when you say it like that."

"Is there another way to say it?"

"Detective, I am here to help these men. I believe there is good in everyone, and I was hoping to find that and nurture it."

"But you do need to work within the confines of the justice system, Ms. Price."

"Missus," the older woman corrected. "And that's what I did. And I think it's what killed Benjamin," she added, frowning for the first time, and lowering her eyes as she shook her head.

"How's that?" Sandoval asked.

"I told Benjamin that the drugs were a clear violation. He understood that would have meant an extension of his time, or even being sent back to prison. I'm afraid that's what pushed him over the edge to do this terrible thing."

"So you think he was so distraught over possibly losing his spot here that he went up to the roof and jumped off?" Sandoval raised an eyebrow.

Price nodded. "Of course, I can never truly know what he was thinking, but I'm afraid it's possible that was why he did what he did."

Jacinta took another drink from her coffee and looked around the office, her eyes settling on the large clock on the wall. "Around what time did you see him last night?"

"I'm not sure, past nine, maybe?"

"It's just before seven right now. How is it you were here so late last night and so early this morning?" she asked.

"I don't really have standard hours, Detective. I try to be here when I'm needed. Last night, I was catching up on paperwork, and I came in earlier than I was supposed to this morning when I heard what had happened. Mr. Sherman called me."

"And the drugs you said Mr. Aubrey was in possession of?" Sandoval asked.

Price's eyes drifted from one detective to the other. Her smile was plastered on her face like a mask. Not even the hint of a slip. "I'm sorry?"

"You said you caught Mr. Aubrey dealing drugs. Did you—"

"Oh! Of course. I have it right here."

Price opened the drawer on her desk and reached inside without hesitation. She pulled out a small bag with white crystalline powder inside and set it in front of the detectives.

"We'll have this analyzed, find out what it is," Sandoval stated, producing gloves and an evidence bag from her jacket pocket.

"Yes, please. I don't want to risk having it in my office any longer."

"Yeah, sure," Sandoval replied, looking at the small bag closely before bagging it and handing it to Jacinta. "So, did anyone here have a problem with Aubrey that you knew of?"

"A problem?" the older woman asked.

"Did he have any enemies? Anyone he'd had disagreements with?"

"Oh, no, nothing I have ever heard about. Is that relevant, though?"

Sandoval's eyebrows raised ever so slightly. "You have a dead man on a fence outside, Mrs. Price. Definitely relevant if he had some enemies here."

"But he committed suicide," Price reasoned.

"Certainly looks that way right now, but we need to cover all bases," Sandoval countered.

"Of course. Well, I don't think Benny had any issues with anyone. He was very well-liked," Price said.

Jacinta handed the bag of drugs back to her partner. "Did he go by Benny in here?" she asked.

"I'm sorry?"

"You've been calling him Benjamin until now. Benny was more of his street name, isn't that right?" Jacinta pointed out.

The smile refused to waver. It was like the old woman was carved out of stone.

"Benjamin, Benny, Ben—" Price shrugged dismissively.

"Right. Well, we've taken up a lot of your time, and we have some more people to talk to. We'll let you know if we need something else," Jacinta stated, getting to her feet. Sandoval got up as well, and the two of them moved toward the door without waiting for the counselor to reply.

"Yes, of course, Detectives. Anything you need."

Jacinta opened the door and headed into the hall, closing it without another word to the older woman. A monitor was waiting for them by the door. He had a radio on his belt, but carried no weapon. Not guards at all, as Sherman had said. Probably an insurance thing.

"You're our chaperone?" Sandoval asked.

"Jack Abbott," the man said, holding out a hand. He looked to be in his mid-twenties, and muscular in a way that suggested if he wasn't at work, he was in a gym.

"Detectives Sandoval and Perez," Jacinta said, shaking the man's hand.

"Sorry if Sherman's been giving you a hard time. He's, uh… well. Just let me know what you need, and I'll make it happen."

"Sherman said he's new here," Sandoval asked. They moved away from Price's office, back down the hall in the direction they had come.

"Yeah, just over a week now, thereabouts."

"He doesn't seem like any warden I've ever met."

Abbott laughed. "As he likes to say, this is no prison. He's an admin guy. I heard that before this, he did finance for the company that owns this place."

"Huh," Sandoval replied.

Abbott chuckled. "Yeah, that's exactly what I said."

"And Price back there? She's not a doctor, right?"

"No. Licensed career counselor, and I think she has a degree in social work? I don't know her well."

"She been here long?" Jacinta asked.

"Yeah. Longer than me, anyway. She deals with residents mostly; doesn't talk much to people who work here."

"That seems weird, doesn't it?" Sandoval said.

Abbott shrugged. "Get the feeling she's one of those holy mission people. No time for the rest of us. She's gotta focus on her goals, you know?"

"Sure," Jacinta answered. "So, how about Benjamin Aubrey? What do you know about him?"

Abbott led them to the stairs and paused, pointing up.

"His room's up on the fourth floor, if you want to check it out?"

"We would," Jacinta answered. He nodded and made his way up.

"We're not supposed to socialize with the residents. They say we're not guards, but then we're tasked with room checks and curfew tracking and all that. But it's hard, you know? You spend hours here with these guys. I knew Benny a bit. He was a funny guy. Real slick, you know? He was a guy who knew everyone else, if you follow me. Connections and connections and more connections."

"You think he was jammed up in something?" Sandoval asked.

Abbott shrugged. "Everyone liked Benny, or they at least didn't hate him. I never saw him causing trouble. Never seemed all that stressed about anything either."

"Did he seem suicidal to you?" Jacinta asked.

"I dunno if it's my place to say anything about that," Abbott replied.

"But I asked. Police business and what not."

The monitor sighed before opening the door to the fourth floor and letting the detectives enter first.

"I got a degree in kinesiology and then criminal justice because I wanted to be a sports attorney, so I'm not really the guy to dig deep into your psyche. But he seemed… cool, you know? He told me once his plan was to get a place, like a real house, and reconnect with his kid."

"But what if he did get jammed up? Like drugs. He could get kicked out of here, right? That could make a guy think dark thoughts," Sandoval pointed out.

"I guess, yeah. But Benny didn't seem like that guy to me. His room's up here, room twelve. His roommate can probably give you more insight if you can get him to be serious for a minute," Abbott told them.

He knocked on the door and stood to one side.

"Hey Cody, got some detectives here who need to look at Benny's stuff. Make sure you got pants on."

"I got pants on, man, come on," came a reply from inside. The door opened a moment later, and a skinny man with a shaved head in gym shorts and a tank top looked out at them, smiling lasciviously. "Man, I woulda been criming this joint up if I knew detectives looked like you two."

"Don't be a jackass, Cody," Abbott warned.

"Hey, man! I'm just being real. What do you want, anyway?"

"Need to ask you about Benjamin Aubrey," Sandoval said, pushing into the room past the skinny man.

The bedroom was small: a pair of double beds, each with its own nightstand and dresser; a shared bookshelf; some wall posters; and a small TV that sat on one of the dressers. It was not a lot bigger than a prison cell, but it was nicer.

"Benny, man, yeah. Hell of a thing, right? Tossed off a goddamn roof," Cody said, shuffling to the unmade bed and sitting on the edge of it. He picked absently at a scab on his elbow while they spoke.

"Tossed?" Jacinta asked.

"Well, yeah," Cody replied. "Benny's not suicidal, man. Guy was working on getting out. Eight months. Everyone here says they're going straight 'cuz you gotta say that to these punks—" he jerked a thumb at Abbott, "—but if anyone could do it for real, it was my boy, Benny. Right, Abbott?"

"Yeah, he could," Abbott agreed.

"So, you don't believe he'd kill himself," Jacinta stated.

Cody made a face and shook his head. "Nah, that's stupid. If anything, he got too cocky, and someone took him out. I dunno what else it coulda been. Or maybe the dumbass just fell off the roof. He liked going out at night, so who knows."

"He often went out at night?" Sandoval asked. She glanced at Abbott.

"They're not supposed to go out at night."

"Yeah. I wasn't supposed to steal that Porsche, but I did," Cody pointed out.

"What did he do when he went out at night?" Sandoval pressed.

Cody shrugged. "We're roommates; I ain't the guy's priest. I didn't ask, he didn't tell."

"How long did he go out for?"

"Not long. Maybe ten, fifteen minutes each time."

"What do you mean by that?" Jacinta asked.

"Huh. It's 'cuz some nights, he'd pop out two or three times…"

"But you don't know why," Jacinta finished.

Cody shrugged again. "I'm goin' straight, keepin' my nose clean."

Jacinta looked at her partner. If Benny went outside a couple of times a night for minutes at a time, he had clearly been back to dealing drugs. They'd have to check the room, assuming Cody hadn't ransacked it already.

She wondered if she'd been wrong to call Shane. It was probably no suicide, but not murder of the supernatural kind either. If Benny had been dealing, he could have crossed the wrong person. But getting him up on the roof and throwing him off with no signs of a struggle just didn't seem efficient. It still didn't make sense.

"Alright, Cody. We're going to need you to leave your room for a bit so we can search it," Sandoval said.

The skinny man smiled. "I got nothing to hide. You do your thing, Miss Detective."

"Just 'Detective' is fine, thank you. Abbott, you got somewhere to send him?"

"Yeah, you got kitchen duty today, don't you, Cody?"

"Me? Nah man, I was in the kitchen last week."

"Well, let me give Burke a call and let him know you're eager for another week. Or you could just head there for today."

"Man, I got you. I got it, I'm goin'," Cody said, heading out.

Sandoval called down for some uniformed officers to help with the search, and Jacinta began going through drawers.

She couldn't shake the feeling her day was set to be a long one.

CHAPTER 4
ARRIVAL

The drive from Nashua to Detroit was about eleven hours for anyone who chose to follow speed limits but was markedly shorter for Shane who did not. Still, it took a large chunk of his day, and it was already early evening by the time he arrived. He had stopped briefly in Canada on his way through. He got something to eat at the same OnRoute rest stop where Wyatt Hawthorn had claimed a couple of his victims. The rebuild looked good.

The stop gave him a chance to read over some of the information Jacinta had texted him after her call. He'd asked her to send him what she knew about the suspicious deaths in the aftermath of the meatpacking plant being torn down.

As she had initially told him, most of the deaths were not particularly suspicious when it came to the details. Early on, there had been one victim in a neighborhood called Petosky-Otsego, a part of Detroit that had fallen on some seriously hard times. A lot of the houses were on the verge of collapse and crime was rampant throughout.

A murder in Petosky-Otsego was not unusual by any means. From what Shane had gathered, violent crimes were a normal occurrence there. But the victim that Jacinta had told him about was a man who'd been a resident at the halfway house for a short time, and had his hand cut off. That was something right up Wyatt Hawthorn's alley. His crimes often ended with mutilated corpses and missing body parts.

But there was one clear difference between the case and Hawthorn's work. For starters, the victim had cut off his own hand—or at least, that was the determination of the medical examiner. The self-inflicted mutilation had led to blood loss, and ultimately, death.

The neighborhood of Petosky-Otsego was not particularly large. There were a number of parks, and it had the illusion of pleasant green space—if you didn't look too hard. The fact that some streets were lined with boarded-up houses detracted from the feeling.

The address Shane had gotten was at the end of one such street, a stretch of road where lawns looked like they hadn't been cut in years, and more than one house was a discarded husk and nothing more. It was hard to believe a neighborhood could look like a ghost town in the middle of one of the most well-known cities in the country, but there it was.

A few people were out and about, and those who were looked like the kind to avoid. Small groups of young men sat on the front steps of rundown houses, and in one case, crowded around a car that looked like it was worth twice the value of the house where it was parked.

Shane parked out front of a house that was only half standing. A fire had burned through the left half, and the remains were scorched around the edges, leaving the building open to the elements. There were weeds growing in what looked like the dining room.

He looked around him and saw that only one house up the street seemed occupied. Everything else looked as though the world had turned and left it there, forgotten and unwanted. There was something disturbing about the idea of dead neighborhoods that was much more off-putting to Shane than the idea of just dead people or even haunted houses.

He approached the burned down house cautiously. The sense of unease was palpable. The neighborhood was dangerous, ghosts or not. He got a feeling from the place that set him on edge. His muscles already felt tense, like his body was already preparing itself for a fight.

There was no door to the building, and after a quick glance behind him, he went in. Inside, the floor creaked and groaned, and each step stirred up dust, dirt, and old, earthy smells.

He moved closer to the burned-out section of the building but paused as the floor softened and squished underfoot. He wasn't interested in taking the risk of falling into the basement. The basement was definitely a place of interest, however. He just needed to find a less dramatic way down.

Little of what remained of the house was noteworthy. What the fire hadn't destroyed, had clearly been looted sometime later. There were walls and rubble and nothing else. Someone had even stripped the wires from the walls and the hinges from the door frames.

Shane made his way through the still-standing portion, until he found a set of stairs heading down into a pitch-black cellar. He pulled out his lighter and headed down.

Like the rest of the house, the cellar was effectively empty. There were piles of trash, evidence people had been sleeping there at one time or another, and the funky smell of mold and sewage. Broken bottles, old cans, and plastic bags were piled up in a corner.

He stood in the center of the space and held the Zippo up to illuminate as much of the space as he could. The air stirred ever so slightly, and the flame flickered. The faint breath of cold danced across his flesh.

"Hello?" he said. No one answered, and he turned around. Under the rotten part of the floor, a figure stood at the edge of the light cast by the flame in Shane's hand.

The ghost was an elderly man with short gray hair and a mustache. He was wearing sweatpants and a dirty t-shirt, and he simply stared.

Shane took a step forward, and the ghost did not move, unaware that Shane could even see him. "Not the nicest digs I've ever seen."

The ghost blinked and cocked his head to one side. "Who you talking to?"

Shane glanced around. "Until someone else shows up, you, I guess."

The old ghost's eyes narrowed. "You see me?"

"Old timer in sweats, real hardcore seventies 'stache? I see you."

The old ghost's face split in a wide grin that showed off surprisingly white teeth.

"Well, I'll be a catfish. You know how long I been here and ain't talked to nobody no how? This is something special. What's your name?" The ghost's fairly monotone voice had taken on a folksy, down-home twist that reminded Shane of an invitation to a family diner.

"Shane," he answered.

"Ah, Shane! It's good to meet you. My name's Carruthers, but you can call me Others, everyone else does. Well… no one talks to me much these days, but you get the idea."

"I get it." Shane smiled. "So listen, Others. Wondering if you can give me some information about your place here."

"This dump? I can tell you that low-rent criminal son of Randall Washington's the one who lit it on fire. Boy grew up to be a bigger piece of trash than his daddy."

"Right. I'm more interested in someone who died here."

"You wanna know what did me in? That goddamn fire! Smoke inhalation, you believe that? I smoked cigars for forty years; never killed me. Then a punk lights my house on fire, and that's it," Others said with a chuckle.

"Sounds like a raw deal."

"'Raw' as a goddamn uncooked pork chop. They didn't even tear the place down after! Just left it here, like a corpse rotting in the weather. Whole neighborhood's turned rotten, from root to stem, if you ask me."

"Yeah, it's looking rough out there," Shane agreed.

"Wish I could just run this whole place into the ground. Turn it all into a park or something, I say. Or a farm. Make it useful again."

"But someone else had died here, right? Fairly recently?" Shane tried to get him back on track.

The old ghost nodded. "Ah, yeah. Gangbanger from the hood. Real piece of work, that one."

"You knew him?"

Others scowled and waved his hand as though pushing the question away.

"Garbage is what he was. Stealing. Dealing. Killing. I seen him out there on the streets. That was even before the neighborhood got as bad as it is. He'd roll folks, steal whatever they had, beat 'em within an inch of their lives. He used the cellar here to stash his stuff sometimes. Saw him kill a few folks, too. Shot a boy point blank for his shoes. His shoes, man! What kinda thing is going on in your head when you kill someone for their shoes?"

"Some people are monsters," Shane said.

Others nodded. "You said it, friend. I say good riddance to him."

"So he did die *here*, in your house?"

"Yeah, he did. You have no idea how scared I was thinking that piece of trash would come back as a ghost, and I'd be stuck here with him for the rest of time."

"I can imagine, yeah. So he got shot here or... what happened?" Shane asked. He knew some of the details already, but he was fishing.

"Nothing so dramatic as that. Damn fool came in here, chopped his own damn hand off, sat down, and bled out. Craziest murder I ever saw, and I seen some things since I been here, let me tell you."

Shane felt the lighter overheating and flicked it off, which plunged the basement into darkness.

"You ain't scared of being in the dark with a ghost?" Others asked.

"You ain't scared of being in the dark with *me*?" Shane asked back.

The old man laughed. "That's a crazy-ass answer."

"So, tell me more about this guy's death. You said he cut his own hand off."

"Sure did."

"Then why did you call it a murder?"

The old ghost chuckled in the dark.

"That's what made it so crazy," he replied. "Come on, let's go upstairs, keep an eye on your car before it gets stolen. And I'll tell you what I saw."

CHAPTER 5
THE MAN WITH NO HAND

It was still early in the spring, and the snow had only just finally gone away. Others couldn't really feel the cold anymore, but he remembered it. Cold was something he hated when he was alive. Now he missed it.

He'd been stuck in the house for too long. Seen too much. But what else could he do? He learned long ago there was nowhere else to go. His lot in life, or death, was to be in that house forever and always. He could walk around the neighborhood, but there was really no escape. Maybe it was what he deserved. He hadn't always been the nicest man when he was alive. Not the best husband or father. Not the worst. But he could have done better.

It was night, and the neighborhood, such as it was, felt as dead as himself. He could spend days standing in one spot, watching the sun rise and set, over and over. Cars drove by; animals wandered into the house. Weeds grew.

And on that night, Lester came back.

Others didn't know the man, but once he'd heard someone call him Lester. He was a thug and a bully, and he had chosen Others' house as a place to do his business. He stashed stuff in the cellar and sold drugs there sometimes.

Others wished he could do something to hurt him, but every time he had tried to touch the man, to punch him or choke him, there was nothing. He had no power to touch the living.

That night was different, though. No deals being made, no raiding his secret stash or beating someone who crossed him. Lester showed up alone, and he looked… off.

Lester carried himself like a big man most times. He thought he was king of the streets and acted the part—strutting around like he was something special, even though he was just a bully in Detroit's dumping grounds.

But that night, he was stiff, unsure of himself. He stopped out front of the house and looked around, as though he wasn't sure what was happening.

Others stayed in the shadows. He didn't know why. It had become a habit over the years. No one could see him, but he still kept out of sight. Maybe it was the shame of what had become of him and the home where he'd once raised a family.

It didn't matter.

Lester came into the house, but it was like he didn't know where he was going. He had been there enough times before, used the place like it was his own. And Others knew then that something was up.

Lester didn't waste a lot of time. He walked to a corner, away from the open front of the house, where anyone could have seen him, and placed his own hand on one of the walls. With no hesitation, he pulled out a cleaver which he had stashed down the back of his pants. One swing, a thud, and boom, he took his own hand off and watched it fall to the floor.

He dropped the knife, then sat down.

Others had never seen anything like it. The man hadn't screamed. He didn't even wince. Took his own hand clean off like it was the most normal thing to do. Blood gushed from the wound, but he didn't care. He just sat and let it happen.

Others had never seen a suicide before, but had always imagined it had to be something more traumatic for the person doing it. But what he saw in Lester was different. No internal struggle. No giving a damn at all.

It only took seconds for Lester to start slouching to one side. Within minutes, his eyes were closed, and he was motionless.

For all Others had seen, and even for all the dark things he'd seen Lester do, he hadn't expected to be watching the man kill himself. He was a criminal and a thug, and he deserved to be punished. But there was something so unexpected and nonchalant about what he'd done to himself.

Others went outside, still unsure what he was feeling after what he'd witnessed. He was only outside for a minute or so, no more than that, but when he returned, he saw someone leaving the house through where the burned-out wall had been. Not a person, though—or not a live one, anyway. It was another ghost. This one was missing most of his face. And it wasn't Lester.

The ghost had either not seen Others, or hadn't cared. He wandered off, and for a moment, Others was confused about how the other spirit could do such a thing. He had tried to leave the house so many times, but had never succeeded. He could go a few blocks in any direction, but he always felt himself being pulled back, like he was on a leash.

When the ghost was gone, Others made his way to Lester. The man's eyes were closed, and in his way, he looked peaceful. The discarded hand lay right next to his body, fingers curved like holding an invisible softball. Blood had soaked into his pants and the dirty floor all around his body.

Days passed before anyone noticed. It was a group of neighborhood kids, out exploring places they had no business exploring, who discovered him.

Others felt bad. Kids didn't need to see things like that, but it was the way of the world around these parts.

Police came. The body and the knife were taken away. And that was it. No one had ever come back to ask or do anything about Lester and his suspicious death.

Not until Shane showed up.

CHAPTER 6
BREADCRUMBS

Shane sat on the stoop in front of Others' house next to the ghost, smoking a cigarette as the sun set. Some of the unsavory types he'd seen on his way had drifted closer to the house and Shane's car, but they were still keeping their distance like vultures waiting for a coyote to die in the desert. He'd have to leave before he tempted them too much.

"So this ghost, you said he had no face?" Shane asked.

Others nodded. "Just the mouth. And it was like… a skeleton smile. Like a caricature of a smile, you know what I mean?"

"I do," Shane replied. That sounded all too familiar. Hawthorn liked to wear a disguise when he killed. He had worn a bandana that covered his mouth with an image of a skeleton's permanent grin. The coincidences were piling up.

But Hawthorn, as a ghost, still had a face. This was something else. Something that knew of Hawthorn. Maybe a partner they'd overlooked. A ghost partner, from the looks of it.

In their initial encounter in Canada, back when Hawthorn had been a living, breathing maniac, one of his victims had returned as a ghost and tried to copy the killer. The two of them had worked at the same time, though definitely not together. Maybe it was someone like that again, someone they'd missed or who had waited for things to die down, before making their own move.

"You look like a man thinkin' thoughts," Others said.

Shane nodded. "That I am. All of this is sounding too familiar."

"You know this no-face fella?"

"Maybe. Hard to say right now. But the details are too close to something else."

He inhaled deeply, then exhaled a puff of smoke.

Others leaned into it and tried to breathe in, then leaned back with a sigh. "Boy, what I wouldn't give for just one more cigar. One puff, even," the old ghost lamented.

Shane lifted his pack of cigarettes and offered him one.

The ghost scoffed. "Get out of here, man. I'd chain-smoke the hell out of that pack if I could, though, not gonna lie."

Shane chuckled, putting the pack back in a pocket and standing up as the last vestiges of the sun faded behind the trees.

"Been a pleasure, Others, but I have some work to do."

"I hear you. No rest for the wicked. Until you die; then it's rest all the time."

With a nod of thanks, Shane headed back to his car. So far, the only thing he knew for sure was that Lester had been at the halfway house, and that a ghost with no face had been involved in the man's death. But Petosky-Otsego was miles from the house. A ghost covering the distance between both would be no easy task. It needed to have its haunted item with it. That meant either a living partner who carried the item with them, or a possession—a living, breathing vessel that could carry the item around. Either way, it required clear planning and intention.

Whoever was killing the people at the halfway house, they were doing so with a purpose. They weren't random victims. Not if Lester was part of the pattern. The killer had tracked that man across town.

That also seemed in line with how Hawthorn had worked as a killer. He stalked his victims, even tracked Jacinta from Canada back to Detroit. He was dedicated and had patience that allowed him to make some remarkably complex—and disturbing—plans.

Whoever the new killer was, they were taking a page from Hawthorn's book, and knew him well enough to mimic some key details. If what Others said was true, and Shane had no reason to doubt the old man, then it was definitely a ghost, as Jacinta had feared. Lots of pieces yet no clear answer to the puzzle. Shane didn't like it.

He pulled out his phone and dialed Jacinta's number.

"Shane! How close to town are you?"

"Been here for a little while. Went to check one of the cases you texted me about—handless guy in Petosky-Otsego."

"What'd you dig up?"

"Ghost here says he saw the murder on the night it happened. Watched another spirit leave, a guy with no face. Just a skeleton's mouth."

There was a moment of silence from the other end of the phone.

"Not a mask this time?" she asked, understanding the significance.

"Just his face. Sounds like he possessed your victim, made him lop his own hand off and bleed out, then left."

"That's not exactly a Hawthorn MO," she said, more to herself than Shane.

"No. But someone who watched him work. Or maybe read about the case."

"You think there's a link? For sure?"

"There's something. But if this handless guy and your suicide at the halfway house are connected, then this ghost has a living partner he uses to move around the city. Whether the partner is a willing participant or not is not clear at this time."

"The house is what links everything. The deaths started there and they're still there."

The street outside was fully dark now. Though there were poles for streetlights, none were illuminated, the bulbs having been smashed out long ago. Shane was in total darkness.

"Sounds like it's the center of everything," he agreed. That meant he'd need to take a look around the building. That was easy enough with the average haunted house he'd run across in his life. Even in a few places where he was clearly unwelcome. But a secure facility meant to house criminals was not exactly the public library.

"We need to get you inside," Jacinta said.

Shane finished the last puff of his cigarette. "Basically."

"This is going to be tough."

His eyes narrowed slightly. "How so?"

"It is a private facility; not run by the state. So, I don't have a ton of clout on access or anything. They work with justice, but they're not really beholden to any agency. It's a contract, just business. So they make their own rules and standards on how to operate, as long as it meets the minimum requirements, they're good to go. And they already know I'm a cop, so there's only so much I can do with my own access."

"Right. So…?"

"So, I'm thinking we maybe backdoor the process. The halfway house and the Department of Corrections cross paths on an administrative level. I know a guy in Corrections. I can get him to set you up for an undercover job. He won't ask too many questions."

"I'm not a cop, Jacinta."

"I know that."

"So, I don't go *undercover*," he stated.

"I can't get you in as just you," she replied.

"I don't need you to get me in. I can find a way in," he assured her.

"For what? An hour? You get caught in there, and it's a felony. That could get you a few years. The place has cameras at the entrance and staff who patrol the halls."

"I won't break in. I'll just go in for a visit."

"You can't just stay in a visitor's room for an hour. You need full access and time to check out the place and the people. There are eighty-five residents, plus staff."

Shane grunted. She was pushing hard, and he didn't like the idea at all.

"I'm not an actor," he countered.

"You don't need to be. Just don't tell anyone why you're really there. Listen, this place just opened a room. I can get you to replace whoever's going to be moving into that room tomorrow. There's no way we can figure this out from the outside. Someone is targeting the people who live there, and we need to get in to stop them."

A flash of movement across the street caught Shane's eye. Too dark to make out much of anything, but he was confident it was people moving closer to him and his car.

He needed to get going. But he needed to reach some kind of conclusion with Jacinta. He was no detective, no paranormal investigator trying to uncover clues like in some TV drama. But she was right about needing access to the inside.

The ghost was in the halfway house, or closely linked to it. There must have been a link between its targets, and the only way Shane was going to figure it out was to be there among them. He absolutely hated the idea of it, but he also couldn't think of a better option.

"I assure you that I am not happy about this," he told her.

"But you also know you have no alternative," she said, and he grunted.

He started the engine and turned his headlights on. A trio of men a couple of houses down stopped briefly, caught in the lights. He smiled at them as he lit another cigarette.

"So, what now?" he asked Jacinta.

"I'll get a hold of my guy. He should get back to me early tomorrow with the details. With any luck, you'll be admitted in time for lunch."

"Detroit is always an adventure," he muttered.

She chuckled. "I'm finishing up a few things with Sandoval. You want to meet up in an hour or so?"

"Give me a call when you're ready."

They said their goodbyes, and he set his phone on the passenger seat. He'd grab a cheap motel room somewhere, the kind of place where no one cared or noticed if he was coming or going at any hour of the night.

He drove off, offering a nod to the gathered group of young men and leaving the ramshackle neighborhood behind him. Ghosts possessing people to force them to kill themselves was rare, but not unheard of. He had to admit it was a creative approach and method of killing.

But the mystery remained.

How was any of it connected to Wyatt Hawthorn?

CHAPTER 7
UNDERCOVER

Shane sat across from Jacinta in a diner, drinking a coffee as she settled in. They had met up the night before, but exhaustion quickly took its toll, and they soon called it a night, their reunion brief and somewhat rushed, with only a short time to catch up.

Jacinta had been up before five in the morning, off to strike a deal with her contact in Corrections. A short time later, she'd made plans for her and Shane to meet for breakfast and arrange his cover. He still hated the idea, but had agreed to it, and would follow through.

Up to that point, he felt that a good part of the reason he and Jacinta worked so well together was the respect and distance they had. Respect for what the other could do, and distance between themselves and that world.

Shane wasn't a cop. For the most part, he didn't even like cops. He knew she wasn't trying to mold him into something he wasn't. She looked at the world in a certain way, and for a detective like her, her approach made the most sense.

For Shane, the idea of kicking the door down and punching people until he found what he needed made more sense. He understood how impractical that was, but it was what had worked for him.

He didn't think that Jacinta's approach was wrong, he just didn't like it, and it didn't suit him. It wasn't his style. But he was willing to admit that it seemed workable.

"Sorry I'm a little late," she told him, waving over a waitress. He sipped his coffee and shrugged. She wasn't really late; no more than five minutes by his count.

Jacinta set a file on the table between them and pushed it toward him.

"This is you. Nothing fancy. You're still Shane Ryan, but as far as Corrections knows, you're working for Detroit PD and going undercover as part of my investigation into the death of Benjamin Aubrey. To that end, you're being set up as Shane Ryan, who's finishing out his second condition on possession charges."

"Possession. Cute," he said, looking at the file.

Jacinta laughed and ordered a cup of coffee and some eggs from the waitress.

"So I'm double undercover? I'm pretending to be a cop pretending to be a convict?" he asked, reading over what she'd given him. It was, as she'd said, pretty bare bones. Possession of meth, tacked on intent to distribute charge, plea deal for reduced sentence, finishing off his time at a halfway house.

"Fewer questions from anyone that way, and easier to pull you out if something goes sideways," she assured him.

"Sideways, huh? Like a ghost throwing me off a roof?"

"I'm sure you'll throw the ghost off first."

"And no one at the halfway house is going to know any of this?"

"They know you as a new resident with a drug charge. That's all."

"Couldn't have made me a crime boss like Capone or something?" he asked.

"No, it needed to be convincing," she teased.

He finished his coffee and nodded as he looked at the scant background he'd been given. He was from New Hampshire; he'd served in the Marines. It was all him. She'd tried to make it as tolerable as possible, which was considerate, he thought.

"What's this?" he asked, pointing to a section on his file that was labeled "work placement." It listed something called Jordan Construction.

"Got you a fake day job. You'll be allowed to leave during the day to go to work, so you can be out during work hours. Anyone asks how you got in, tell them it's your cousin's company."

"Sounds like you're setting me up long-term here," he pointed out. The waitress arrived with coffee and filled a cup for Jacinta, then gave Shane a refill.

"Just in case. How long do you think this will take?"

Three, four hours, he thought. He didn't say as much, though. Truth be told, he had no idea. He could legitimately end up in the halfway house for days, even weeks. A ghost that didn't want to be found could be very hard to root out. The only ace up his sleeve was the ghost not knowing anyone was looking for it.

"As long as it takes," he answered.

"Insightful," she told him. "Just remember, this isn't sanctioned anywhere across the board. Corrections thinks this is being run through the local police department; the halfway house thinks it's run through Corrections. At some point, there will be an accounting error if we don't close it out, and that'll bite both of us in the ass."

"Accounting?"

"For-profit, remember?" she reminded him. "They're expecting to be paid to house you, so you have until the monthly invoice is due to find out what's going on. Or, to put it another way, you only have to endure this until the invoice comes due."

He smiled at that, watching her put sugar and cream in her coffee. She knew he didn't want to do the job this way, so it was some degree of comfort to know it couldn't go on for too long, regardless of what happened. A built-in expiration date was a nice touch.

"When am I going in?" he asked.

Jacinta looked at her watch. "You're scheduled for a ten o'clock arrival."

He looked at his own watch and frowned. That didn't leave a lot of time at all.

"Keep your eye on a counselor named Jocelyn Price. Got a weird vibe from her. And the administrator is weird, too, but I checked his story, and he's only been there for a week or so."

"Possessions aren't the easiest thing in the world. Victims have to have an opening that can be exploited. Depression, addiction, mental illness, something like that."

"Then a lot of people in a place like that are vulnerable."

He nodded. A halfway house was probably prime ground for finding people who would be vulnerable to a ghost. Especially a determined one.

The likeliest scenario was that the ghost had latched onto one particular person. Possessing one person made it easier to really burrow in like a tick. And if the ghost was moving in and out of the facility, then it had to be someone who had the ability to do the same without attracting too much notice. Staff members, like Jacinta said. Guards, counselors, administrators. Any of them could have fit the bill. So that would be his focus. He'd shake a few branches and see what fell out.

They finished their breakfast together as Jacinta offered a few more details of what she had arranged and how things worked at the halfway house. Her friend would drop Shane off, so there was no connection between him and Jacinta to rouse anyone's suspicions. His day job was set up to start right away, and the paperwork was ready to go through, so he didn't need to worry about any red tape. And, as she'd learned off the record from her contact, the halfway house was sloppy about the actual legal aspects of it all, so it was unlikely anyone would dig deep enough to find discrepancies or issues. Certainly not before Shane was already out of the place and the task was done.

Shane checked out of his motel and left his car at Jacinta's. She drove him back to her station and parked in the lot behind the building, next to a beat-up gray sedan from the early eighties. A thickly built man with a crewcut and sunglasses waited next to it, leaning on the trunk.

"Ryan?" the man asked as Shane and Jacinta approached him. He extended a meaty hand.

"Yeah," Shane agreed, shaking.

"Paul Lo Truglio. Perez here tells me you're looking into the W Four C. I told her there's been something fishy going on there since it opened. Glad to see someone finally doing something about it."

"You've had suspicions about this place before?" Shane asked.

Lo Truglio scoffed and looked at Jacinta for a second. "This guy. Yeah, since—what's his name, Dayton?"

"Tom Dayton," Jacinta confirmed.

"Since Tom Dayton got collared for drug trafficking. Using residents in the house to move it. You could say I've been suspicious."

"Dayton being…" Shane began.

"The previous administrator, yeah. Place has a shady history, and with all the deaths, we're just trying to connect some dots," Jacinta said to Lo Truglio.

"Alright. Well, you do look like a con, buddy, I'll give you that. Maybe more of a lifetime mob enforcer than a drug guy, but I ain't complaining."

He laughed and clapped Shane on the shoulder, walking around his car and opening the back door.

"Appreciate the vote of confidence," Shane said.

Lo Truglio laughed again. "Alright. They're expecting delivery in a few minutes. I got your paperwork faxed in already, and they'll give you the room assignment and all that jazz on site. You need me for anything, you give me a call. They're pretty lax about phone rules there so no one should give you a hard time. But fly under the radar as much as you can; I heard some of the monitors are hardasses."

He handed Shane a business card, then headed around to the driver's side door. After slipping the card into his pocket, Shane stood next to the car for a moment.

"Good luck," Jacinta said with a grin on her face.

"I can't wait to get this over with. I'll settle in, have a look around, and meet you somewhere tomorrow."

"I'll keep digging into the victims, see if there's a deeper connection we're not seeing." She glanced at Lo Truglio. It seemed like she wanted to say more, but didn't, in the interest of keeping up the ruse that Shane was indeed a member of law enforcement going in on an assignment. Instead, she waved goodbye as he got into the back of the car.

Lo Truglio drove his ramshackle car like he was being chased by the police. Shane found it oddly comforting that the man was so confident in his skills that he would be so reckless.

The approach to the halfway house was familiar to Shane, and he remembered the neighborhood from his previous experience with the meatpacking plant.

From the outside, it looked like a small apartment complex, with white framed windows and dark brick. The grounds were surrounded by wrought iron fence and young fir trees that blocked most of the outside world from view at street level. There were no signs outside, and nothing to indicate what it was for. There wasn't even a number on the outside wall or the gate to indicate the address.

Lo Truglio parked next to a "no parking" sign and got out, circling around to let Shane out as well. They walked up the paved path to the front door and entered.

The facility had a strange smell to it, somewhere between cleaning products and cafeteria food. A man sat at the front entrance desk with a sign-in book and a computer in front of him. Lo Truglio flashed his ID.

"Got your new transfer here," he told the man.

The man at the desk, wearing khaki pants and a polo shirt, typed something into the computer. "Shane Ryan?"

Lo Truglio nodded. "Yep. You good to take him off my hands?"

The man scanned him computer, pursing his lips, and clicked on a few things. "Looks like we received the orders and processed him already. Yeah, he's good to go."

Lo Truglio nodded then faced Shane. "Alright. Welcome to your new temporary home, Ryan. Don't screw up."

Shane nodded. He assumed convict Shane Ryan would have little to say to Lo Truglio, so he said nothing. The other man left, and Shane remained still in front of the desk.

"So, Ryan," the man at the front desk began, "I've got your room assignment, and I'll have a monitor come to show you around shortly. For now, let me reiterate that Wayne County Community Correctional Facility is not a prison; it's a transitional residence designed to help you bridge the gap between prison and society…"

Shane listened as the man recited what was clearly a rehearsed introduction probably given to every single person who walked through the door. Most of it sounded like PR and marketing nonsense, with the barest hint of lip service to the idea of rehabilitation. It probably played well with politicians and investors. None of it mattered, so he mostly tuned it out, instead focusing on the small details of what he could see around him.

The place was meant to house former inmates who were in the process of reintegration, not a five-star hotel. And it did have an air of cheapness to it, though it wasn't falling apart. The faceplate on a plug outlet was slightly crooked, and some trim along the floor had been set with sloppy cuts. Little details, but ones you notice when you're trying to ignore a long-winded speech.

"Understood?" the man at the desk asked as he finished his spiel.

"Got it," Shane replied. He had heard most of the words, and was confident he had the gist. Curfews, work rules, random drug tests, that sort of thing.

"Great. I'll just need to take your things for routine inspection, and welcome to W Four C," the man said with a sincere enough smile that mildly surprised Shane.

"Thanks," said Shane, handing his duffel bag to the other man.

Now he just had to keep the whole ruse from collapsing before he found his ghostly murderer.

Piece of cake.

CHAPTER 8
THE BELLY OF THE BEAST

"Bedrooms are all on floors four and five," Jack Abbott said, leading Shane down a hallway on the fourth floor. They'd covered the kitchen, the dining hall, the therapy rooms, the common room, the yard, the administrative wing, the classrooms, the workrooms, and every other inch of the building. He had been undercover for all of an hour, and he hated it already. There was so much useless ground to cover.

The only thing he had observed was that the ghost was not loitering the halls. The other residents had looked him over the way tough guys looked over everyone new, and the guard, who insisted he was a "monitor", had been tolerable, if not boring. He seemed like a straightforward man, though, not one of the difficult types that Lo Truglio had mentioned before.

"You're going to be sharing a room with Clem Bridges," Abbott told him as they approached the end of the hall. Shane said nothing but did note that neither Jacinta nor Lo Truglio told him he'd have a roommate.

"Sounds good," Shane said.

Abbott laughed. "Yeah. Wait till you spend a day with him. Anyway, schedules are posted on the bulletin board downstairs, as well as every entrance and exit, and on the back of your door. You miss a meal, then you miss a meal, so don't do it. No outside activities after sundown; that includes the yard. Spot checks can happen any time, so no contraband in your room. No fighting, no spitting, no breaking anything. Only water is allowed in your room, no colored drinks. Make a mess, clean it up. Respect the process and you get respect. Break the rules, we'll send you back upriver. Good?"

"Good," Shane replied. They stopped in front of a door, and Abbott knocked once, then opened it without waiting for a reply.

The room was small, like a college dorm. One bed was unmade, with a stack of folded linens on top, along with Shane's bag. The second was half made and cluttered with various clothing items, an empty bag of chips, and some other trash. His roommate was not present.

"Clem, what's up?" Abbott shouted into the room.

"Toilet!" came a muffled reply.

Abbott shook his head. "Got your new roommate here. Show him around, don't be weird."

"Got it, boss!" came the reply.

Abbott turned to Shane.

"Take some time, settle in. We got about a half hour before lunch. I'll see you down there."

Shane nodded as Abbott left him alone.

The interior of his new room was not messy, but not tidy, either. Clem's housekeeping style seemed chaotic. Books were stacked on a shelf sideways. Some were graphic novels, some looked like seedy romance novels, and there were a handful of ragged-looking Stephen King titles as well.

Clem's dresser drawers were all closed, save for one which had two pairs of underwear and a single stray sock. Shane was not encouraged.

He checked his own drawers next to his bed. After monitors had searched through them, his clothes had been brought in ahead of him, and it looked like someone had dumped everything in a single drawer. He set about making his own bed.

"Roomie, you there?" the voice from the bathroom yelled.

"Yeah, here," Shane answered.

"Hey! I'm Clem! I'm your roommate!"

"Yep, so I heard."

There was a rustling sound, and the toilet flushed. The door squeaked on rusty hinges, and a thin man with the paltry scraps of a beard appeared. He had bags under his eyes, and his arms were laced with tattoos. One of his front teeth was missing, but he smiled broadly.

"Hey! I'm Clem!" he said again, holding out an unwashed hand.

Shane nodded, holding up his sheets. "Shane," he replied.

"Cool, Shane!" Clem made a fist and bumped it against Shane's hand. "This is great, man. I haven't had a roommate in a while, and it gets boring up in here, no joke."

"I bet," Shane grunted.

"What you in for man?"

"Possession with intent to distribute," Shane answered, fitting the sheet on his stiff and stale-smelling mattress.

"Yeah, they get everyone on that, man. You wanna know what I'm in for?" he asked then. Shane continued making the bed.

"Shane, man, you wanna know what I'm in for?" Clem asked again, sitting on his own bed.

Shane suppressed a sigh. "What are you in for?"

"Complicity, man! You ever heard of that? Complicity!"

"You were an accomplice?" Shane suggested.

Clem laughed. "Hell yeah! I drove the car, that was it. Never even robbed no one. Got a nickel for it. Crazy stuff. But now I'm here, so that's cool, right? We're 'transitioning back to normalcy'. That's what the Black Widow says. I'm down for it."

Clem was a lot to take in, and Shane was almost convinced Jacinta was playing a joke on him. If people hadn't died, he would have been sure of it.

"Who's the Black Widow?" Shane asked. He had the sheets pulled tight, military corners, and smoothed out the blanket on top.

"Price, man. You'll meet her after lunch for group counseling. Just a warning, as a new guy, she's gonna single you out."

Shane looked over his shoulder. Clem was now rearranging the books on his shelf in a different, but still disorganized way.

"How's that?"

"Man, she'll make you introduce yourself and talk about what you did, why you're here, and what your goals are. It's like middle school, man. So awkward. But she will not let you off the hook. Best to power through."

"Why do you call her the Black Widow?"

Clem chuckled, then grimaced, looking toward the doorway before taking a step closer.

"Everyone does, man," he whispered. "She's like this sweet old grandma but then, you know, get close to her and you die."

"She kills people?" Shane asked with some skepticism. There was no way it was going to be that easy.

Clem laughed. "Man, you're crazy! She's like, a hundred years old! She don't kill people. I mean, like, yeah, she kills people. But not like... come on, man, you know?"

"Clem, you're losing me," Shane said.

Clem waved his hand, as though wiping away everything he'd already said. "I'm just saying, man. This dude, Benny, he just died, like this week, and he was one of her cases. Before him was Tuck, and before him was Manafort. Like, she starts counseling them then they off themselves. That's crazy, right?"

"They commit suicide?" Shane asked.

Clem grimaced in a comical fashion. "That's what they say. But it's just weird. It's happened too many times in the past months, is all I'm saying."

"No one's looked into it or anything?"

"Man," Clem said, turning away to busy himself with his disorganized shelf once more. "I'm saying, it's not like she really kills people. Nothing to look into, right? But at the same time, you know, don't go on the roof with her, like Benny did. Or take pills—that's how Tuck went down. Or, ya know, strangle yourself with a sheet in the shower. That was Manafort."

Shane nodded in response. An elderly woman would have trouble doing those things to anyone, but not a ghost. A counselor would be a reasonable possession choice, but Shane wasn't sure they'd be the best for getting close to convicts in a halfway house. Did criminals get close to career counselors? He had no idea, but it seemed like a violation of some kind of professional ethics.

"Anyway, man, you look like you know how to take care of yourself, but stick with me in here. I got your back," Clem told him, sitting on his bed again. Shane sat down as well, pulling out a cigarette. His roommate grimaced again and shook his head.

"You'll get bathroom duty for a week if they catch you smoking in your room, man."

Shane stopped with the cigarette halfway to his mouth. "You for real?" he asked.

Clem nodded solemnly. "You bet. But dig this, man, there's a shower fan for getting moisture out of the room. You turn that on, and you can smoke under it. No one will notice."

Shane lowered his hand. "You want me to smoke in the shower?"

Clem shrugged.

"Just saying, man. Best way to do it if you don't want to get caught. Otherwise, you'll need to go downstairs in the yard."

Shane put the cigarette back in the pack and considered the quickest way he could get his job done. Clem was probably not going to be much help. It was a question of how much he might hinder Shane, especially if he needed to do anything after hours.

"I'll keep it in mind, thanks," Shane said.

Clem grinned, showing off his missing tooth. "Not for nothing, man, but if you need *something*, then maybe I know some ways you can get access to stuff you might want to have on the inside."

"Stuff, huh?" Shane asked.

Clem shrugged. "Whatever you need. I can get it on a good turnaround. And I mean that, man. You want, like, a hot piece, I can do that. Just lemme know."

"Alright," Shane said. That was potentially useful to know. Not that he needed anything from Clem, but it did mean Clem was likely the kind of guy who could keep a secret. Might come in handy down the line.

"My best advice is to get a job as fast as you can and stay outside as much as possible. This place sucks, man, straight up. Like, it's super boring, and counseling is super boring, and some of the monitors think they're in Rikers, you know?"

"I got a job already, so no worries there."

"Get out, man! You got a hookup that fast?"

"My cousin's construction company," Shane explained.

Clem looked impressed. "For real? That's cool. You get outside for full workdays? I only work part-time. And hey, they give you travel time, too. You know, like for dental and all that. Or your kid's birthday. You can go places and everything if you're quick."

"I'm probably just working," Shane assured him, sensing there was an unspoken request in there somewhere.

Clem waved his hands and shook his head. "No, man, for real. I get it. But when Sugarman hears you're out and about, he might hit you up for a favor."

"Now who's Sugarman?" Shane asked.

Clem leaned closer to him and lowered his voice again. "I'm the guy who can get you, like, a Blu-ray of your favorite movie or a burner phone. Sugarman is the guy who can get you, you know, other stuff."

"Other stuff," Shane repeated.

Clem nodded very slightly. "I don't like to talk shit about no one, alright? And you didn't hear this from me at all, but Sugarman is not a dude

I'd deal with. If I was you."

"Appreciate the heads-up," Shane told him. Sugarman was a dealer, and based on the marked shift in tone from Clem, not a friendly one. That was the kind of person that a ghost could make use of. Much easier to frame, as well. No one would dig too deep if someone like that was involved in something like murder.

"Listen, man, it's close to lunch. You wanna get down there early, in case they run out of the good stuff. Sometimes the kitchen guys double down on servings for their boys, and you end up with a plate of steamed vegetables or some garbage like that."

Shane stood up and followed his new roommate out of the room. There were a couple of other open rooms with residents inside, chatting with each other or reading, one even playing chess by himself. Nothing stood out to Shane, and everyone was alive.

They headed down a different set of stairs than the ones Shane had used to go up, on the opposite side of the building. The long, narrow stairwell made their steps echo loudly up and down the distance. At the third-floor landing, Shane felt a subtle but noticeable drop in temperature.

He stopped at the door and opened it, looking out into the hall.

"Wrong floor, man. We're going down to the first floor."

Shane nodded, saying nothing. The third-floor hallway was empty. It was lined with offices, and the doors were all closed as far as he could see. The chill in the air remained even as they continued down to the first floor.

The third floor looks like a good place to start, Shane thought as he followed Clem down to the dining area.

CHAPTER 9
MEETING EVERYONE

Lunch at W4C was not something Shane was looking forward to repeating again. He'd hoped he'd left flavorless food with suspect ingredients in the past in foxholes and cramped quarters in miserable corners of the world, where you ate what you had to eat to survive. The fact that Clem had identified some of it as "the good parts" was equally concerning.

Shane scanned the room silently, enduring the chatter from Clem and a handful of others they had sat with after some perfunctory introductions. The other men they ate with were a mixed bag. One guy was in for a financial crime that was straight white collar, while another had been boosting cars. Shane wasn't sure how the facility ended up choosing residents, or what someone had to do to qualify to be placed there, but it didn't matter.

No one seemed suspicious yet. The other men introduced themselves and chatted and shared jokes and news of the day. There was gossip and rumors and talk about the man named Benny who had died. Like Clem, the others were convinced that Jocelyn Price was bad news.

"I don't get it," Shane said, eating a plain piece of bread and butter. "You say this woman is old, like grandmother old, but you all think she's somehow involved in the deaths of these guys? How?"

Emmitt, the car booster, was in his late twenties. His nose had been broken so many times that it was nearly flat on his face now. He shrugged, shoveling what the W4C staff had said was beef stroganoff into his mouth.

"You'll find out soon enough. She's next level. No one is as nice as her. No one. But you listen to her, especially one on one, and it gets really unsettling."

"What does that mean?" Shane asked.

"She drops these digs at you. Like how maybe you'll be better off back in prison. Maybe you're not cut out for this program. Maybe she'll have to write you up. But then she pulls back on it. She'll scare you, then ease off. It's emotional blackmail if you ask me."

"Why would she do that?"

"Hell, why does anyone do anything around here? Manipulation. Torture. Powerplays. It's not any different from prison."

"Just figured it'd be different here, I guess," Shane said, trying to sound convincing.

"Only difference is this place is privately owned. It's a business," Emmitt said with a laugh. "You'll see as you get to know her. Do I think this old lady lured Benny to the roof and asked him to jump off? Hell, or pushed him off? No. I don't think she had a damn thing to do with it. Not directly. But she gets in your head, and I could see that breaking a guy down after a while. The way she toys with people is weird."

"Has anyone ever filed a complaint about her?" Shane asked.

Clem laughed so loud it startled the room, but he reeled it back. The other guys laughed as well, chiding Shane, which he tried to accept with good grace, and meant resisting the urge to pop everyone in the teeth.

"You're new here, guy, and I get it, but woof, bad take," Emmitt said. "Anyone tell you about Dayton, the guy who used to run this place?"

"Drug Trafficking?" Shane said. Emmitt nodded.

"Yeah. That man was running this place like he was Scarface. So no, no one has filed a complaint about anyone here. And the new guy's a complete dumbass, in case you're thinking management style is any better these days."

"Sounds like an every-man-for-himself situation," Shane

suggested. Emmitt chuckled.

"You got it, man," Clem replied. "You just gotta stay under the radar, that's what I say. You'll make it through." He turned to the others then. "My man's already got a job lined up, you believe that?"

"For real?" Emmitt asked.

"His cousin got him in his construction business. My cousin Philly's doing more time than me, man," Clem replied.

"Lucky guy," Emmitt stated. Shane smiled, finishing up his meal despite the taste.

The conversation drifted from one random topic to another for the next half hour, until it was time for group counseling. Shane had been lumped in with Clem for his first day and after bussing their trays in the kitchen, the two of them headed down the hall to the therapy room.

Group counseling took place in a mostly empty and nondescript room featuring only a circle of chairs. There were thirteen chairs in total, so a dozen participants plus the counselor leading the session. Several of them were run every day, Clem explained, to ensure everyone was included, and to work around schedules for residents who had outside jobs.

Counseling took place daily, and it was mandatory. They covered what people had done at work if they had jobs, the job hunt for those who had none, and various self-affirming and motivational things that all sounded remarkably uninteresting to Shane.

A handful of residents were already in the room when Shane and Clem entered, and so was a woman who looked more out of place than anyone Shane had ever seen in his life. She wore a blue and yellow sweater, and her snow-white hair was pulled up in a bun. She had to be in her seventies and was slight and small—the exact opposite of intimidating.

The woman's eyes fell on Shane, and for a moment, they simply regarded one another in still silence. She looked away soon after, and spoke to a man about moving a chair, then went and poured herself a cup of coffee from a carafe.

Shane felt nothing in the room and didn't recognize anything about her at all. But a possession was not something he could easily see through. If a ghost was hiding in her, then he needed to wait for it to exit its host before he'd know for sure. He was suddenly reminded of the Canadian he'd met previously.

Surely could use Big Bear's powers right now.

More men filtered in, and once the seats had been filled, the woman clapped her hands.

"Okay, gentlemen, welcome. I see we have a new face today," she said, smiling widely at Shane.

Clem nudged him in the ribs. "Power through, man," his roommate whispered. Shane grunted.

"I am Jocelyn Price. You can call me Mrs. Price. Or Jocelyn, if you like. I am going to be your counselor here, and as I'm sure you've heard, we have these little meetings every day. How about you introduce yourself to the group," she said.

"Shane," Shane said.

Price blinked and waited for him to continue, but he did not. Some of the other guys snickered.

"Shane. Okay… nice to meet you, Shane. Care to give us a little more? What brings you here?"

"Drug charges," he answered.

"Okay, drugs. Lots of other residents here have walked that road, so no strangers here. I used to be an addict myself, which you probably don't know." The woman's smile had not slipped at all during their interaction, and it struck Shane as unusual.

"Okay."

"I must say, you don't seem like a user to me," Price said, almost under her breath, as she sorted through some files in her lap. "Okay, yes, I see now. Transferred in this morning. Two convictions for possession. Twelve months left to be served here. Isn't that something?" she said.

"I suppose so." Shane shrugged.

"Well, Shane, I think you are going to fit in well here. I see you even have a job lined up already, and that's great news. That's what we're striving for. Hard work that pays dividends and gets us all back into the world again as responsible citizens."

She sounded like she might break into a cheer at any moment. There was nothing about the woman that stood out as wrong—yet somehow, everything stood out as wrong. She was too cheerful and supportive. Shane disliked her.

The rest of the counseling session was as mundane as Shane had expected it to be. Price maintained her cheery and supportive demeanor for everyone there the whole time.

She said or did nothing suspicious during their time together, but of course, Shane hadn't really expected her to. The others mentioned it was more of a one-on-one thing, and even then, they still acknowledged that she was not directly doing anything suspicious. He knew he had to wait until they were alone to gauge how she acted.

The counseling session ended, and the men filtered out of the room. Price lingered a moment and approached Shane as Clem was explaining the easiest way to get to the yard.

"Shane, it was a pleasure to meet you," Price said.

Clem backed off and Shane replied, "You too."

The woman locked eyes with him, and her smile continued unabated. "I'm glad you're here with us. I look forward to seeing what happens next."

What happens next? What the hell does that mean? "Well, you've got me for a year," he told her.

She nodded, and her smile finally shifted. Her lips closed, and she no longer showed her teeth. "Yes. A whole year. Who knows what progress we'll make?"

With that, Shane watched her leave the room, unsure how to interpret the interaction. Was she weird? Most definitely. Was she possessed by a killer ghost? He didn't have a clue. And he certainly didn't have a year to get to the bottom of it.

Clem walked with Shane out of the room, and they headed down a long hallway lined with windows. Shane stopped midway down towards their destination.

Outside, across the street from the house, was a park. He vaguely remembered it from his last time in Detroit. But now, as he gazed out the window, he caught sight of a man under one of the trees, simply standing still and not doing anything. His eyes were focused on something Shane couldn't see, and he stood like a statue.

The front of the man's shirt was soaked red, seemingly covered in a spray of blood. But no one else in the park had noticed. No one else could see him.

It was the first ghost Shane had seen all day. If he was at the park, there was no reason to doubt he could get in and out of the W4C premises as well. And Jacinta had mentioned the earliest deaths had been in a park close to the plant.

It was a potential lead. But he needed to get to the park without anyone thinking it was unusual. And he wasn't cleared to leave the grounds until the following morning for work.

"Hey, roomie, you good, man?" Clem asked once he realized Shane had stopped.

Shane nodded, pulling out a cigarette and placing it between his lips. "Just checking out the view," he said.

"Of Dead Man Park? Okay," Clem laughed. Shane glanced at him, the unspoken question on his face, and Clem nodded out the window.

"There'd been like a gang war or something a little while back, but I wasn't here yet, I don't know a lot of details. But they say everyone got all sliced up on a bike path in the middle of the day. Rumor has it, they don't do a lot of charity walks through the park anymore these days because of that."

"Oh," Shane muttered. The ghost definitely looked like he had been in a gang.

He could be one of the victims. He'd have to remember to check it out in the morning on his way to "work".

Clem led them around to the back of the building and into a green space that was fenced in and surrounded by trees. A couple of other guys were already smoking out there, and another was reading in a lawn chair. Shane lit his cigarette and took a deep breath in.

"This is just a backyard," he stated.

Clem nodded. "Yeah, man, didn't I tell you we were goin out to the yard?"

"Yeah, but... I mean, no one ever hops the fence?"

Clem laughed. "To what? Escape? We're not on death row, man. You want to be *in* here. This is your ticket out. Only an idiot would try to take off from this place. If you do want to do something that's against the rules, you just do it under the radar. You're allowed to go in and out. Go to job interviews, that kind of stuff. So you go do your approved time out business, then find ways to get your other business done before coming back. Easy peasy. No need to jump fences."

"Good point." Shane took another puff.

Clem nodded at the cigarettes in Shane's pocket. "You got a spare, man?"

Shane exhaled smoke from his nose and raised an eyebrow as Clem smiled.

"I'll pay you back, man. You know where I live!"

Clem's attempt at an endearing smile fell flat, but Shane acquiesced nonetheless, pulling out a single stick and handing it to the other man.

"I knew I'd dig you, man. We're gonna be good roommates," Clem told him, lighting the cigarette. Shane grunted again.

He was overjoyed at the prospect.

Chapter 10
The Black Widow

The rest of the day went painfully slow. Clem was not wrong about W4C being boring. There was TV to watch, books to read, and games to play, but none of it appealed to Shane. He was not interested in poker with snacks as stakes, or exercising with a jump rope in the hot, smelly gym.

They returned to the cafeteria for dinner, and it was slightly more palatable than their lunch had been. Their entrée was chicken and rice, and it resembled what it was supposed to be. Though the limp and flavorless steamed vegetables proved Clem's point about not wanting to get stuck with a plate full of them.

After dinner, Shane stayed with Clem while he socialized with Emmitt and some of the others. Shane himself had little to say, but he was trying to blend in, and that meant sitting there and nodding along when necessary. It was frustrating at best.

He had spent most of his time smoking when he found the chance and realized his pack was nearly empty. He went out just before sundown to finish it off. He'd have to hit up a corner store before talking to the park ghost the next morning.

Already making plans, he thought. That was something.

The yard was empty when he went outside. The sun was low, and he was still within curfew. But it seemed like no one else was interested in cutting it so close. He stood in the yard and stared at the trees, smoking in silence until he heard the door behind him open.

"Getting close to curfew, Shane."

He knew who it was even before he faced in her direction. When he faced her, he saw Price standing in the doorway with that same smile. He held up a half-smoked cigarette between two fingers.

"Almost done," he said.

She gestured to his hand, the missing fingers. "Were you in an accident?"

He nodded. "Just carelessness. It was a long time ago."

"Carelessness can get the best of us, can't it?" she said. He took another drag on the smoke.

"Hopefully your days of being careless are behind you. I was just reading your file today. Your history is with drugs. Hope you've learned your lesson there."

"Oh, I have." He gave his own fake smile.

"That's good. And you're working in construction, correct? Is that what you did before getting incarcerated?"

"I've done a lot of things," Shane replied, not wanting to commit to anything.

"It's good to have purpose. That's what keeps us all rooted and on the right path, I think. Do you agree with that?"

"Sure." *Man, she is weird.* He sensed that she was trying to imply something that she wasn't willing to say out loud, but he had no idea what it was. It was like she was working at an inside joke, only no one else was around to appreciate it. It was easy enough to see why Jacinta and pretty much everyone in the halfway house felt uneasy around her.

"Sun's nearly set. You best head in now. Wouldn't want anything bad to happen on your first day here," she said with a laugh.

Shane nodded and finished his cigarette, fieldstripping the butt before heading into the house.

Price held the door for him. Her strange smile stayed firmly on her face as he shifted sideways to get past, staring her in the eyes as he did so.

He'd never had to interact with a person in the strange, forced way Price took towards everyone. Though her behavior was suspicious, he was starting to wonder if she truly was possessed or was just socially awkward.

If the ghost's goal was to sneak in and out of the premises undetected, it did not make sense to act so strangely. Maybe the ghost simply didn't care or wasn't even aware of how they were coming across.

But if indeed Price was possessed and the ghost inside her wasn't worried about getting caught, then that could be a bigger problem. It meant the ghost felt it had nothing to lose. It knew none of its victims could escape from their current position. That would allow it to be bold, and even more dangerous.

Shane brushed past as politely as he could and began down the hallway, ignoring the older woman.

"Have a good night, Shane," she called after him, not leaving the doorway.

"Good night," he replied.

Shane made his way to the stairs and up to his floor. He passed other residents on the way, some heading down and others milling about. Most just watched him go, cautious about a new face in what was not quite a prison.

Clem wasn't in the room when Shane arrived, which was a spot of relief. His roommate wasn't the worst person Shane had ever met, but if given a choice, he never would have picked to live with the man in a million years, even temporarily.

He knew he needed to find a way to move around the house that didn't arouse suspicion. Lurking about on his first day would probably draw too much suspicion. He resolved to stay in his room for the night and see what he could do the next day.

By the time Clem returned to the room, it was close to lights out. He regaled Shane with tales of a board game he'd been playing and tried to get Shane to promise he'd join the next day, which he refused to do.

After Clem had been silent for about twenty minutes, and Shane had assumed he'd fallen asleep, he asked, "So, you feeling this place?"

"Feeling?"

"Yeah. You got a good vibe here, or no? Some guys just can't transition from being in lockup to this place. They get like a weird kind of cabin fever or something. It's rough. Gets ugly."

"No, nothing like that. It's fine," Shane told him.

They were both in their beds in the dark. Lights from the street filtered in past the edges of ill-fitting window blinds, and Detroit's white noise droned in the distance.

"I think it'll be good for you. You're not a big talker, I get that. But you got a good start with a job already. I seen this place change lives, man. It's worth it."

"You think this place will change your life?" Shane asked.

Clem laughed in response. Shane could hear him roll over on his bed.

"Hell yeah, man. And I want to change my life. If I hadn't been picked up on that accessory collar, I'd probably be dead by now. Two guys I used to run with got shot a month after I went up. A month. And those were my boys. Something like that happens, you'd get this urge, you know, to do bad. To like… I dunno, to get back out there and get revenge. But I had time to work past that. I don't want revenge anymore. I just want to live, man. To survive. Turn things around for good. Make sure my mom doesn't have to worry that I'm next, you know?"

His voice was breathy as he spoke, the topic getting him worked up. Not in an angry way, but with an almost childlike excitement. As a result of his incarceration, he saw a future for himself.

Shane was not inclined to feel a lot of sympathy for a guy like Clem, but everyone had their story. Whatever Clem did to end up in prison was in the past; no one had a pristine road of virtue and Shane didn't expect anyone to. But if the guy saw a brighter tomorrow, with the halfway house being the first step toward it, that was a good thing.

"I get it." He really did. His own past had been a winding road, sometimes not of the best choices.

"Yeah, man," Clem said after a satisfied sigh. "I get a good vibe off you. I think this place will be good for both of us. Maybe we can meet up outside of this dump for a beer one day."

Shane almost laughed. Clem was certainly a trusting and friendly person. He wondered if that was how he'd been roped into being a getaway driver in the first place.

"Sounds good," Shane agreed, hoping it would shut Clem up. He wanted some rest. He needed to get to the park ghost, learn what he could about Jocelyn Price, and get the hell out of the W4C as quickly as possible.

"Cool. See you tomorrow, Shane," Clem said, rolling over again. Shane grunted and waited to see if there would be a follow up. There was none.

Five minutes later, the soft sound of Clem breathing deeply filled the room. Shane closed his eyes and let sleep take him.

✴

Shane's eyes opened with a start. As he sat up, his hands were already balled into fists. The room was pitch black, save for a sliver of yellow light that cut past the blinds and illuminated part of Clem's side of the room.

He sat still, listening to the night. There was no sound in the room and no movement that he could see or sense, but he had heard something. A thump, muffled somewhat. It was the sound of something being thrown or dropped, he was sure. Something bulky, but not too hard, nothing that crashed or banged. More like a heavy bag. Or a person.

The silence stretched on, and Shane glanced over at Clem's bed. The covers were tossed to one side, and his roommate was gone.

Carefully and silently, Shane got to his feet. The bathroom door was open, lights off, and there was no sign of Clem inside. The man had left the room.

Shane held his breath for a beat, just listening. Beyond the faint drone of the outside world, there was nothing to hear. His own room was as silent as a grave, and Clem was definitely gone from their quarters.

He reached for the doorknob and began to turn it slowly and purposefully. Outside, overhead lights illuminated the hallway with a soft yellow glow.

Shane blinked at the light, and his eyes moved immediately to the only thing that looked out of place in the otherwise empty hall.

Clem was on his back, eyes staring blankly up at the ceiling. A trail of off-white foam ran from the corner of his mouth to the floor next to him, where it had pooled into a small puddle. There were white fragments in it, chunks of something that looked vaguely like pills.

Shane stared down at the man, and felt a faint chill in the air slowly dissipate. There was no doubt in his mind now. It was a ghost. But the fact that it had chosen Shane's roommate was something else entirely. It could have been a coincidence, but Shane didn't believe in coincidences. Not in a situation like this.

Whoever the ghost was, it used Clem to frame him and take him out of the picture.

It was safe to assume the ghost knew who Shane was and what he could do.

CHAPTER 11
LEVELING UP

"What time did you discover the body?" the monitor with the ponytail asked.

Shane shrugged. "Didn't check my watch. It was about ten minutes before I called you guys," he answered.

Ponytail's scowl was pronounced. "Ten minutes? Why'd you need ten minutes?"

"I didn't need ten minutes; I took ten minutes. Clem wasn't going anywhere."

Shane was in his room with Ponytail and another monitor, Duncan. Police had been called, as had an ambulance; not that the latter was going to be of much good. Clem was very much dead.

"You think this is funny?" Ponytail asked.

"Am I laughing?"

A red flush creeped up the monitor's face.

"Did you see anything?" Duncan cut in.

Shane shook his head. "I was asleep."

"So you just got up and walked out of the room, into the hall, and found your roommate dead?" Ponytail asked, his tone suggesting he believed something else had happened.

"Yeah. I heard a noise; I got up and checked."

"What kind of noise?" Duncan asked.

"A thump," Shane replied. "Found Clem on the floor. Saw the vomit, checked his vitals, and realized it was too late to help. Came back in here and took a piss."

"You went to the bathroom before calling for help?" Ponytail asked incredulously.

Shane shrugged. "I had to go."

"Where'd he get the drugs?" Duncan asked, redirecting the conversation again.

"How should I know?"

"He was your roommate," Ponytail stated.

Shane chuckled and looked at his watch. "Yeah, for about nineteen hours. I didn't know the man. I didn't know what he was into. You probably knew him better than I did."

"Then you'd be okay with us searching your stuff." Ponytail said.

"I just got here yesterday. You literally searched my stuff, and I haven't been outside since," Shane reminded him.

"You have a lot of attitude for someone whose roommate just died," Ponytail pointed out.

"Why don't you leave the interrogation to me, huh?" a new voice chimed in.

Ponytail turned to Jacinta, who was accompanied by a uniformed officer and a pair of paramedics, who immediately went through the motions of checking the very dead body of Clem for pulse. The uniformed officer began to usher Duncan and Ponytail from the room.

"We're just gathering some information regarding the crime, Detective," Ponytail replied.

"Oh, is this a crime scene? Didn't realize you were so far along in your investigation. That's great," Jacinta said to him. "The two of you can wait downstairs, and if I need you, I'll come find you." Her tone suggested she was not interested in discussing the matter further.

Duncan glared at Ponytail and nodded that they should leave. Ponytail glared at Shane for just a moment, then made his way out of the room. The uniformed officer followed them.

"Mr. Ryan, right?" Jacinta asked Shane, noting that the trio was still within earshot.

"Yes, ma'am."

"Not even one day in here," Jacinta said in a lower voice.

"Not my choice," he answered. "Where's Sandoval?"

She sighed and entered the room then closed the door behind her.

"She's heading to the prison Clem transferred from to talk to his ex-cellmate. I convinced her that it made sense to attack this from two sides."

"She'll be ecstatic to see me," he told her.

Jacinta smirked. "Well, hopefully you're out of here before she catches wind. Just easier that way. So, what the hell happened?"

Shane shook his head. "Guy's a low-level criminal. Drove a getaway car or something."

"Yeah, I checked his record before I got here."

"Decent enough guy, though he talked too much. Had a normal day with him. A loud thud woke me up at around four o'clock. Checked the hall and found him like that."

"With no one else around, of course."

"Just a really cool breeze," Shane said, making eye contact with Jacinta.

She frowned. "Right. Have you met Price? What do you think of her?"

"Weird," he told her. "She's off somehow."

"Possessed?"

Shane shook his head. "Maybe. It's hard to say. People here call her the Black Widow. People around her die too often, looks like. But she's obviously not pulling the trigger herself. I gotta get closer, see what I can figure out."

"And you definitely don't think Clem committed suicide?"

"For sure. He was waxing poetic about this place changing lives and second chances and that kind of stuff earlier. He seemed genuine. He wanted a fresh start after getting out of here."

"Right," Jacinta said, looking around the room. "Once the medical examiner takes a look, I have a strong feeling this is going to be a straight-up suicide, real cut and dry."

"Most probably," Shane agreed.

"But it was an overdose, and that's going to be our in. Whoever's behind this did that think of that. Drugs are supposed to be hard to come by in here, especially after the former administrator's crimes. So someone messed up, and that means more scrutiny on this place. Means more freedom for me to dig into things."

"Clem told me who I can go to for stuff like that. A guy the call Sugarman is apparently the hookup for drugs."

"*Sugarman*? Why not just go by 'drug dealer'?" Jacinta asked.

Shane chuckled and shook his head. "Yeah, well, that's his nickname."

"Okay. I can use him as an excuse to further the investigation as a potential murder. You keep an eye on Price. She's not on-site right now, but the guys downstairs told me she was on the way in."

"She's been chatty with me. I don't imagine it'll be hard to stay on her radar."

"Chatty?"

"Suspicious, I suppose. She read my file. Stopped me last night to talk alone, but nothing too overt. She "found" me outdoors right before curfew, used the chance to make small talk."

"Well, I don't need to say it, but watch your back."

"Always," Shane replied.

"Any insight into why your roommate was targeted?"

"Just one idea."

Her jaw clenched, and she nodded very slightly. "You're thinking your cover is blown."

"After, like what you said, not even an entire day of being

here. Someone recognized me right away."

"But how?" she asked.

He shook his head. "Won't know until I know. So they have the upper hand right now."

"I can get you pulled from here right now," she offered.

Shane pondered it for a moment. As much as he hated the idea of being undercover, and as much as it was clearly useless for tricking a ghost, it was necessary for the access. The ghost was in the halfway house. And it had intentionally not attacked him. Like far too many ghosts, it was trying to be intimidating or frightening. That meant it was ignorant, arrogant, or both. That was something he could work with.

"No. The ghost is here. This—" he pointed toward where Clem had been found, "—confirms it. It'll be easier to find if I'm on the inside."

"It'll be easier to kill you, too," she warned.

"Have some faith," he chided.

Jacinta laughed, though not with much conviction.

"Alright. But call me if things fall apart in here. I'll do what I can on my side of things, make sure this ghost knows the spotlight is on this place."

"I have a lead. I'll let you know if anything comes up," he said.

She opened the door again and looked out into the hall. A photographer was just finishing taking pictures of Clem's body. They removed him shortly thereafter, while Jacinta left to do her job elsewhere in the building. Shane was left alone in the room.

Within a half hour, a monitor Shane didn't recognize arrived to clean Clem's vomit off the carpet.

Shane stared at the spot where he'd found his roommate. Clem didn't deserve to die, but if there was an upside, he had the room to himself now. That meant a little more freedom to come and go without anyone wondering what he was up to.

Killing Clem was meant to send a message—Shane was sure of

that. But going for Clem instead of him was a mistake. The ghost was not smart, certainly not as smart as it likely thought it was. That was going to be the tipping point. That was something to exploit.

Shane lay back on his bed and stared up at the ceiling. Clem's untimely death made him eager to start the day—to hopefully find and destroy the ghost before he'd need to spend another night in the room.

CHAPTER 12
DEAD AND UNBURIED

The sun was just rising when Shane awoke again. Time had passed without more attacks and a sound out of place. He readied himself for the day and headed downstairs to find some coffee.

Other residents whispered among themselves, and a few came to ask him about what had happened to Clem. He told them what he had seen and nothing more.

Abbott came to him as well and asked about the night's events and he shared the story once again. The monitor was suspicious of the idea that Clem would overdose in the hallway. He seemed to be the only employee in the entire house capable of thinking beyond the superficial.

Shane's workday was meant to start at eight o'clock, so he finished his coffee and some toast with as little fanfare as possible, and left before anyone else sought to engage him in conversation. He signed out at the front door and provided the necessary information for where he'd be, including the fake number Jacinta had given him for the job.

There was no sign of Jocelyn Price as Shane made his way from the building, out onto the street. He made his way to a store at the corner and bought a new pack of cigarettes. Vaguely remembering the front desk monitor's rules and reminders from the previous day, he asked the store clerk for his receipt before heading to the park.

He lit up a smoke and stood on the sidewalk for a moment, inhaling and taking a moment to just *be* outside. Even if his time in the halfway house was technically voluntary, it didn't feel that way. It felt like prison.

Shane scanned the park that sat opposite the W4C. It was not large, but there were enough places and trees for a person—living or dead—to hide if they were crafty enough.

He headed down a walking path toward the center of the park. People were on bicycles or walking dogs, and a few were sitting on benches having their morning coffee, heads buried in their cell phones.

Close to the far side of the park, Shane caught sight of the ghost he was looking for. His back was to Shane, and he sat on the edge of a small retaining wall near a tree. His short blond hair was stained red from the cascade of blood flowing down from a gaping wound in the top of his skull.

Shane approached him at a leisurely pace, rounding the path until he was alongside the retaining wall. He sat down next to the ghost and raised the cigarette to his lips.

The ghost glanced at Shane and he offered a nod in return.

"I'd offer you a smoke, but I don't think it'll do you much good."

The bloodied young man stood up quickly. He was probably twenty at most and had the look of a kid who thought himself both tougher and smarter than he really was. His sneakers looked like they probably cost close to a thousand dollars.

Instead of speaking, the ghost locked eyes on Shane for a moment, then slowly leaned forward and waved his hand in front of Shane's face, as though testing a blind man's ability to see.

"That's a new one," Shane remarked.

"You can see me," the ghost whispered.

Shane nodded. "Yep. You look terrible, by the way."

"How? No one's been… I haven't talked to anyone since—"

"Yeah. Most people will never see you. But some can."

"You need to tell my mom! My brother! Can you get me out of here? I can't leave the park. I tried, but I kept coming back. I need to go—"

"Hold up, there," Shane interrupted, putting his hand up. "I can't take you out of here if this is where you died. Something of yours is keeping you here; that's how it works."

The ghost cursed and turned in a circle, frustrated for a moment. "Can you tell people I'm here?"

"No," Shane answered.

The ghost made a face, something close to indignance. "What do you mean? They need to know I'm still here!"

"But you're not," Shane explained. "Your spirit is, but not you. You died here. Your family or friends, whoever you left behind, they've said their goodbyes. How long have you been here?"

"How long? It's been… I don't know. Just before they've torn down the meatpacking plant. We were… My buddy, Kendall, stabbed me. I never even knew why."

"Seen anything weird around here since you've died?" Shane asked.

The ghost stared at him blankly. "Weird?"

"Yeah, did you see anything? What about the suicides at the halfway house?"

"What suicides?" the ghost asked and Shane nodded. "I saw a guy take a dive off the roof the other day. That was no suicide, though. Looked like one if you weren't there, I guess."

Shane took the cigarette from his lips and looked back towards the house. It was almost impossible to see from where they were located.

"What makes you think the guy didn't really jump?"

"He wasn't alone," the ghost answered. "I was on that side of the park. Sometimes I hang out by the road. I tried getting out of here but I couldn't. It's like I get pulled back to this spot once I reach a certain point? Does that make sense? But I take walks, especially at night when the park is closed, you know, just to see people. So I go over there to watch people walking down the street or driving or whatever. Makes me feel like

I'm a part of the world still, sorta."

"So you saw him with someone else on the roof?" Shane asked.

The ghost shook his head. "Not exactly. I only saw him after he fell. But he wasn't alone. There was a ghost with him. No, more like, in him."

"*In* him?"

"Yeah, saw the ghost as he left the guy's body."

Damn it. So, a possession. When will this end? Shane thought. Out loud, he asked, "What did this ghost look like?"

"He looked... horrible," the ghost replied. "He didn't really have much of a face. Like he had a face, but it was blank except for his mouth. It looked like a skeleton's mouth. No eyes, no nose, none of that."

"Did he do anything?"

"Just went back into the building. Like he was going to work or whatever."

"Was that the only time you saw this faceless ghost?"

The ghost made a face and shook his head. "No, I've seen him a bunch of times. Not daily or anything, but pretty consistently. I'd see him go inside sometimes, moving around the neighborhood other times. Not sure where he goes though, and to be honest, I don't want to get close enough to find out."

Shane finished the cigarette and looked around the park once more before looking back at their limited view of the W4C.

"Why don't you want to get closer?"

"Did you not hear what I said? He doesn't have a face, just a skeleton mouth. That's creepy as hell."

Shane grunted. "Okay. But you're dead, too."

"Yeah, but I have a face still. I'm not like a ghoulie or whatever that guy is. Plus, it looks like he kills people. What if he also kills ghosts? Not even sure if that's possible, but what if? I already got killed in life. Don't wanna die a second time."

"Fair enough," Shane said before changing tack. "There's a woman who works there. Elderly, small, with white hair, looks like she weighs nothing. You ever see her around?"

"Yeah, I sometimes see an old woman coming and going," the ghost said.

"You see her that night, with the dead guy?"

"I didn't. She's usually like most people, in and out, to and from work. Keeps odd hours, I guess, but that's it. Is this, like, a murder investigation or something? Are you like, a ghost cop?"

"No," Shane said, without explaining any further. On a few occasions, he had been called a Ghostbuster, too. People, and ghosts, got too much into writing their own little stories about his life.

Shane stood then, checking his watch. His fake workday had barely started. He needed to touch base with Jacinta to see if she'd learned anything new about Clem or the Aubrey guy.

"If you see anything else, I'm staying over there for now. Give me a heads up?" Shane asked.

"You're a con?" the ghost asked.

"A man's gotta have hobbies." Shane winked as he started down the jogging path again. "Anyway, I appreciate the info."

"Wait!" the ghost called, joining him as he continued to walk. "You're just leaving? We gotta tell people!"

"Tell them what?" Shane replied.

"About me. About ghosts! Everything. You could change the world. You can talk to the dead!"

"Oh, that. No thanks."

"No thanks?"

Shane pulled a new cigarette from his pack. "Not the kind of ride I'm looking for."

"But you have proof of an afterlife! You could be rich!"

Shane grunted and kept walking. New ghosts were certainly a naïve lot. He'd have time to grow into the full realization that life after death didn't have a lot of upsides to it. Certainly not many for a living person trying to pull back the curtain on it. That'd be a quick way to either get committed or killed, not to mention all the unwanted attention.

"Seems like a fun idea until a ghost like no-face over there gets mad and kills me for blowing the lid off things," Shane suggested.

The other ghost raised his eyebrows and nodded after a moment's thought. "Oh. Yeah, I guess maybe some people want it to be a secret."

"Let me know when you see anything. Thanks."

The park ghost nodded. "Yeah, sure. Come back anytime. We can talk about anything," he said. Shane raised a hand in acknowledgement and continued on his way.

He left the park behind and traveled a few blocks before settling in at a diner. He hadn't eaten a real meal in a while, not a decent one anyway, and it would give him a chance to plan his next moves. He ordered a coffee and sat in a booth before calling Jacinta.

There was something strange going on, and he'd get to the bottom of it if it killed him.

CHAPTER 13
THE DARK PLACES

"Off to work?" Jacinta asked when she answered the phone.

Shane took a sip of surprisingly good coffee and shrugged. "Nose to the grindstone. Got news for you."

The diner was a simple hole-in-the-wall. No '50s theme or anything of that nature; just a sort of no-frills, poorly lit space that smelled of coffee, seared meat, and fried food. He liked the atmosphere.

"So do I," she replied.

"You go first," he offered, having another sip of the coffee.

"Got preliminary results on Clem's vomit. Unchewed chunks of alprazolam. Xanax. And checked the W Four C medical records for residents. He never had a prescription," Jacinta said.

"Yeah. Maybe someone inside has a prescription. Or other means of access," Shane suggested.

"Looking into it," she replied. "What's your news?"

"A ghost in the park across the street. He watches the house sometimes. He's seen the same faceless ghost that the one I met in Petosky-Otsego had seen. No eyes, no nose, just a skeleton mouth. Says he's seen it going in and out of the house for a while now."

"How is this faceless ghost involved in the deaths?"

"He saw it by the jumper's body, right after he jumped."

"Great," Jacinta said with some degree of sarcasm. "Now we just need to figure out who it is, where it is, why it's doing this, and how to stop it."

"We will figure out a way to stop it and where it is, more or less," Shane reminded her. "The other two… not really that important."

"You don't want to know who this is?" she asked him.

He shrugged, finishing his coffee. "It's gotta be someone with a connection to Hawthorn. This all started after I destroyed his ghost. And he'd been in the process of perfecting his twisted art. This ghost has no face. An unliving monster, like the corpse spider he put together. So maybe this ghost was phase two. A practice run that worked out but stayed in the background until Hawthorn got put down."

"Maybe," Jacinta agreed.

"That's why it's unimportant. At the end of the day, I still need to get rid of whoever it is."

"This is crazy. I wish there was a way to make this easier. Make it less dangerous."

"If it were easy, then everyone would do it," Shane joked.

"Well, even if you're not that interested in knowing who this ghost is, I am. I'm still trying to connect the dots. He's in that house, hiding in plain sight, and I want to root him out."

"Nothing connects your victims together beyond the house? Or to Hawthorn?"

"Nothing. The only connection I see across the board is the house itself. It might just be that simple. They're in this place together, and our killer is just taking whoever is convenient."

"Could be that easy. Ghosts aren't always deep thinkers about this sort of thing."

"I'll keep looking and let you know if I turn anything up."

"I'll do the same," Shane said. "One thing, though. The first deaths, the ones in the park the day Hawthorn was destroyed. Any of those guys got stabbed in the head?"

"Um…" He heard her clicking keys on a keyboard for several seconds. "Yeah. Killer slit his own throat, but he did stab one of the others through the top of the head."

"Yeah, I think I've met him today. He wasn't a resident at W Four C."

"No, they were low-level street dealers. Some say it was probably a deal gone bad."

"So that one doesn't fit the pattern at all. No connection to the halfway house."

"But still in the immediate area," Jacinta remarked. "And they all have shady backgrounds.

"Right. So, what if the halfway house is just a convenient source of victims? Like a trout farm for a fisherman."

"Which makes our theory of Hawthorn being linked stronger."

Shane grunted in agreement. "I'm going to see what I can dig up on my end; I might have an idea. I'll let you know later."

"Right. I'm checking on Jocelyn Price, too. Text me if you find something."

They said their goodbyes, and Shane put his phone away. He understood Jacinta's compulsion to want to answer all the questions, to root out the mysteries of who, where, when, and why. For Shane, it didn't matter at all. When the house is on fire, you don't stop to ask why it started; you just put it out and worry about the details later. The faceless ghost had to be stopped and the rest was just a distraction.

Something the ghost in the park had said was already setting Shane on a new course of action. He needed some kind of lead, and the ghost had told him that the faceless ghost came and went frequently. If the halfway house was its base of operations, then it wasn't going far. So he had a range that he could investigate, a sense of where to look. Even if he didn't find the ghost, he might be able to find where it was spending its time other than the house. Or someone else who had seen it.

He paid his check and left the diner. He couldn't be seen loitering around the W4C during the day, but as long as he avoided the building itself, he was likely to go unnoticed. His best bet was sticking to side streets and alleys to see what he could turn up.

Shane doubled back the way he had come, then began weaving along the side streets. While the immediate area was mostly industrial and commercial, the next blocks over were residential areas.

The neighborhoods looked quaint, and not nearly as rough as Petosky-Otsego. Some houses were a bit worse for the wear, but many were average homes that blended into average streets.

Nothing stood out as Shane walked—certainly no sign of anything dead and menacing, but no sign of much of anything. Most of the homes were quiet, the residents likely gone to work for the day, and only a handful of cars passed him on any of the streets.

As he headed west of the W4C, the neighborhood began to grow a little more downtrodden. More than one home was boarded up or in a state of disrepair. Most homes still looked like they were occupied and relatively well-maintained, but the instances of abandoned homes became more frequent. But there were no signs of ghosts around.

Shane reached close to what he assumed was about a mile from the halfway house, then cut left. The new street was far worse than the one he'd been on. A number of lots were empty; some with houses that were recently razed to the ground while others had clearly been empty for a while. At the corner, he found what was once a small bodega-style store, the front obscured by an unkempt overgrowth of weeds and trees and a dirty sign that read "Pop Shop".

In the empty lot next to the shop, a half dozen children were playing a ramshackle soccer game, using a pair of trees as goal posts. The children all appeared to be under ten years of age, and none of them seemed afraid of the nearby empty building, despite the ominous air it projected.

Shane walked around the building, giving it a closer inspection. The door and front windows were all boarded up and laced with graffiti, all looked like they had been done some time ago as well. There was a second floor, and the windows up top had not been boarded, but they had old newspapers taped over the glass from the inside.

There was nothing from the outside that necessarily indicated the building had anything wrong with it—not more so than the other abandoned buildings in the area. But still, something drew Shane toward it.

"You're not supposed to go in there," one of the children yelled at him as he made his way around the side of the building. They had stopped playing, and some of the kids dispersed after seeing a stranger checking out the abandoned shop.

"Says who?"

"Everyone. It's condemned. It's probably full of stuff that'll give you cancer."

The boy was thin, looked even thinner in his oversized yellow hoodie. He seemed more confident than most children his age. He was the only one in the group who didn't seem immediately suspicious of or fazed by Shane's presence.

"Probably," Shane agreed.

"Andre! He's a cop. Don't talk to him, Andre!" another boy in a basketball jersey shouted.

Andre waved him off. "He's not a cop. Look at him. Probably just robbing the place." Andre turned back to Shane. "There's nothing to rob in there. It's been boarded up forever."

"Well, that's alright. I'm not looking to rob it either," Shane told the boy.

Andre's expression grew suspicious. "Are you here about Tug?"

"Is that a person?" Shane asked dubiously. The boy scoffed.

"Tug used to run this neighborhood, man. He was like the Godfather."

Shane arched an eyebrow, mildly surprised a boy as young as Andre had seen *The Godfather*.

"Used to?" Shane asked instead.

89

"Yeah. Everyone else thinks those guys from the south side took him out."

"But not you?"

"No. I saw him go into the Pop Shop the day before he went missing. He was stashing stuff in there or something, I dunno. But I was in the field here the last day anyone saw him, and something pulled him back in. I told everyone the Pop Shop ate him, but no one believed me."

"It *ate* him?"

Andre shrugged. "Yanked him right in like it was sucking up a noodle."

"And you're still playing out here in the field after witnessing something like that?"

"I ain't getting close enough to get ate!" It was sound logic for a child.

"Have you ever heard anything in there?" Shane asked him.

Andre nodded. "There's a TV on sometimes, I think. Really quiet though. You going to check it out?"

"I think so," Shane told him.

Andre scoffed again and shook his head. "Your funeral, my man."

"Andre!" the other boy yelled again. Without another word, Andre left, joining his friend and leaving Shane alone.

So, you eat people, huh? Shane thought, returning his attention to the building. There were no windows along the side wall leading to the rear, and the back door had been completely sealed over with wood.

He followed the edge of the building, pushing the underbrush and overgrown weeds aside. To the far side of the boarded-up door, a small basement window had been smashed in. Boards that had once covered it were removed and had long since been covered with weeds and grass.

Crouching down, Shane peered into the darkness beyond. The basement had a damp smell to it and was almost completely lost to shadow. What he could see in the small patch of light from the window was scraps of wood, broken glass, and rocks on a cement floor.

With one final look around, Shane got down on his stomach and lowered himself through the window. The air was cold once he was inside, and somewhere beyond the musty, earthy smells that filled the place was another scent that was too familiar.

The place smelled like death.

Chapter 14
The Ghost Upstairs

The basement of the Pop Shop had likely been looted ages ago, if it ever had anything of value in the first place. There were empty boxes and cheap, rusted shelving that had been pushed over. A handful of broken bottles filled one of the corners, but nothing remarkable stood out in any way.

Despite the lack of anything noteworthy, there was a feeling to the place that set Shane on edge. He'd been in too many places that had the same feeling. Hell, his own house had it; the sense that something was not right.

And that he was not alone.

A set of wooden steps in the center of the basement led up to the main floor. He had no direct evidence there was a ghost present, but the feeling of the place, combined with Andre's story, made it seem more than likely.

The wood groaned under Shane's weight, ensuring that if he had any element of surprise, it was no longer present. The second step was worse than the first, but he powered on. Having the upper hand would have been nice, but there was nothing he could do about that.

At the top of the stairs, the door had just been lazily placed in the frame, not even attached at the hinges. Shane moved it aside, giving him access to the backroom of the store. Wire shelves lined the space, and more empty boxes and plastic crates that had once held milk.

Shafts of daylight crept in through cracks in the boards over the front windows. The main part of the store had been gutted, with only the front counter and some shelves left. The rest was just trash, and signs that someone had once tried to live there long ago.

A blanket and a filthy pillow were caked in dust and cobwebs. There were cans of food around the makeshift bed, mainly soup and potatoes, and they were all just as dusty. The floor showed signs of more recent life, however. Clear signs of rats, but also prints from boots and shoes, some old and some fairly recent. The newer ones did not venture into the store. Instead, they led to another set of stairs that went up.

Shane had guessed that the second floor of the store was an apartment. There were many similar setups in Nashua as well. Store owners lived upstairs and worked down, saving some cash on rent and utility bills. The upstairs would likely be a full apartment, then.

The second set of stairs was not as loud as the one in the basement, but there was still a low, noticeable creak as his weight stressed the wood on each step. He didn't bother to hide his ascent.

At the top, another door hung open. It led to a small entryway with a set of coat hooks fixed to the wall and some old pizza boxes piled in the corner. A smear on the wall could have been paint or food, but the pattern and the familiar brownish-red tone were too hard to mistake. It was blood. Very old blood.

Shane entered the apartment, which quickly gave way to a living room. To his left, there was another doorway; to the right, the living room merged into the kitchen. He would have investigated further, but there was no need.

The living room was still in relatively good condition. Less dust than the lower floor, but still more than any living person would accept. The corners were dressed in thickly layered cobwebs, and there were small piles of old trash, like cans and bottles and cardboard boxes here and there. A coffee table in the center of the room still had a couple of magazines on it.

On the wall farthest from Shane was a small table and a television that had to be thirty years old. It was on, and a sitcom was playing. Wires that looked hastily spliced together ran from the television through a hole in the floor to somewhere below.

Opposite the TV setup, an old, rust-orange sofa covered in dusty pillows was placed against the wall.

The ghost who sat on the sofa was huge. He was shirtless, and his broad chest and back belonged to a man who had spent the better part of his life in a gym. His shoulder muscles were nearly the size of Shane's head. He ignored Shane and watched TV intently, despite there being no eyes in his head.

A laugh track erupted from the TV, and the ghost chuckled as well.

Shane took another step into the room. "Good show?"

The ghost turned his head, brow furrowing over what looked like fresh, bloody wounds where the man's eyes had once been. "Huh?"

"Nice set up you got here," Shane said. He hadn't met many ghosts who watched TV to pass the time.

"Yeah, I guess so. This place is mine, though. You can't stay."

"I'm not here to move in."

The ghost turned back to the TV. "What you here for, then?"

"Are you Tug?" Shane asked.

"Bolo. You here for Tug? Then you're not going to like what you'll find." The dead man grinned but remained focused on the television.

The smell of something dead was stronger inside the apartment than it had been downstairs. Shane had no doubt what had become of Tug.

"Just heard he came in here once. Actually, I'm more interested in someone else. A ghost."

Bolo's eyeless face turned to Shane. "You see ghosts, huh? Not many people got that skill... What ghost are you looking for?"

"From what I've been hearing, he's a faceless ghost," Shane told him. "He frequents a halfway house a few blocks from here. But also roams the neighborhood."

"Yeah," Bolo said, looking back at the TV. "I know him."

"You got a name?"

"Nah," Bolo said. "You got a beef with that ghost? Forget it. It's not worth it."

"Just trying to figure out who it is and what he wants," Shane explained.

"No, you're not," the big ghost said. "You got a beef with him. I smell it. You want to stop him? Confront him? Dumb idea."

"Why's that?"

Bolo shook his head. "He's good. He's working for good. So you should let him work. Leave him alone."

The answer was not one Shane had been expecting. Most ghosts would have gone in for a little ominous melodrama. Threats and promises of the bad things that awaited Shane if he wasn't careful.

"What good is he doing?"

"You been outside. You saw the neighborhood," Bolo began. "That look good to you?"

"It's a little rundown—"

"Run down?" Bolo scoffed. "It's dying. Half dead already. Cursed. People here aren't living, they're barely surviving. You got drugs, robbery, murder. Worse things sometimes. It's like a sickness. Spreads all over."

"Okay…"

"No one does anything anymore. Let something rot for too long, and it seems hopeless. But not this guy. He's cutting out the rot. He's doing good."

Shane nodded, realizing what the ghost was saying. "Because he's killing criminals,"

"And making things better."

"So, is he blaming the people he's killed for this neighborhood falling apart? Does he think killing one criminal, or ten, makes him a hero?"

"No!" Bolo exhaled loudly. "It's not just one man's fault. Not one problem. It's the system. The culture. Pick up one gangbanger and put 'em to prison, that's a Band-Aid solution. The problem still remains. We work differently. Cut out the disease before it causes more problems. Here. Elsewhere. Doesn't matter. And the effect spreads. To this neighborhood. To your neighborhood. The whole world, one day. Get rid of the thing that causes the problem, then there's no more problem."

Shane put a hand in his pocket, feeling the iron rings inside. If Bolo was correct, the faceless ghost fancied itself some kind of vigilante. Killing criminals to prevent future crimes. That was not what he'd been expecting.

"You said 'we'. You helping this other ghost then?" Shane asked.

Bolo nodded. "This is my town. My home. I can make it safe again for good people. Make it safe for families."

The big ghost turned away from the TV again, his empty eyes seeming to look right through Shane. "I did bad things once. I got punished for it. They made me watch my family die. Then they took my eyes," he said. "But now I can do right. I need to do right."

"I appreciate that," Shane replied. "Atonement's a big thing for some of us. So, is this your idea, or the faceless ghost's?"

"His idea. He found me after I saw him one night; made me see things his way, and I agreed with him."

"Has he got a name?" Shane asked.

"We call him Death's Head. I saw him take control of a man, made him kill himself. Never knew we could do that."

"He taught you about possession."

"Not at first. He didn't trust me. But we talked. He told me what he was doing. What I could do. He made me see how my choices got me to where I am. How I could make better choices now, even in death."

"He sounds like a real life coach."

Bolo frowned. "It's not a joke. He knows how we can change the world in ways we never could have when we were alive."

"But it involves killing people," Shane pointed out. "Which you said was part of the problem. Murder is still murder."

"Not the same," Bolo suggested. "These aren't good people. I've been here my whole life. I was here when this was a good place. Pop ran this store. Everything was good. Good neighborhood. Good people. But the industry shut down, and the jobs all left, and things got bad. People got bad."

"Still not seeing how that makes killing people the solution."

Bolo smirked and shook his head. "It's because you're thinking small. Think bigger and you'll see. I couldn't save anyone before. Couldn't save my brother. Couldn't save this place. But I can do stuff now, and that will change things around here. That's better than doing nothing, isn't it?"

"I get the idea, sure," Shane said. "I just don't see how you fix a crime problem by committing crimes. That's not how this is supposed to work."

Bolo laughed. "That's funny. You're funny. How things are supposed to work. My parents weren't supposed to get killed. My brother wasn't supposed to get killed. You gonna yell at the guy shooting you that it's not how things are supposed to work?"

"So, you guys just figure a halfway house is just a good hunting ground for bad people?"

"It is, don't you think?"

Shane could feel the tension rising. Bolo was relatively calm, but the words he spoke made him seem like a zealot. If Death's Head was recruiting ghosts to some kind of perverted justice crusade, he could have a full-blown cult on his hands. That was not something Shane wanted to deal with.

The sound of his phone ringing drew Shane's attention. Bolo simply turned his attention back to the TV.

Tentatively, Shane pulled the phone from his pocket and saw Jacinta's name on the screen. With his eyes on the ghost, he pressed the green button and raised the phone to his ear.

"Shane?" Jacinta asked.

"Yeah," he replied.

"Can I speak with Bolo, please?"

He held the phone to his ear in silence for a moment.

"Are you still there?" she asked after a beat.

It was her number on the phone, her voice in his ear. "Yeah. But how—"

"Put me on speakerphone, please."

"Jacinta?"

"Speakerphone. Please," she insisted.

His muscles tensed as he felt his heart begin to pump faster, adrenaline already coursing through his veins.

He did as Jacinta asked, lowering the phone and pressing the button for the speaker.

"Am I on speaker now?"

"You are," he replied.

"Bolo, can you hear me?" she asked. The ghost tore his eyes from the TV, looking towards the phone in Shane's hand.

"Bolo, it's me. Kill this man. It's for the greater good, I'm afraid."

The phone clicked, and the line went dead.

CHAPTER 15
LIFE OR DEATH

Bolo lunged at Shane, wasting no time. The phone fell to the floor as Shane ducked aside, avoiding the ghost's first attack. As big as he was, Bolo proved to be nimble and fast.

A massive hand caught Shane from behind as he tried to duck aside, lifting him from the ground.

Shane attempted to turn and retaliate, but the big ghost's movements were swift and fluid. As quickly as he had snagged Shane, he spun and released him again, throwing him across the room and into the wall above the sofa.

The drywall crunched under Shane's weight. A great flurry of dust fell free as he crashed onto the sofa. Bolo didn't hesitate and came for him again. Shane's reaction was more desperation than calculation. He kicked, aiming low, and slammed the heel of his foot into Bolo's left knee.

The ghost had clearly never been in a fight with a living person capable of fighting back. If he had been alive, his leg would have fractured and crippled him. As a ghost, it was worse.

A combination of the force of the blow and the momentum of the ghost separated Bolo's shin from his knee. It was like breaking a breadstick.

Bolo cried out, more from rage than anything else, as his leg came apart. He tumbled forward, catching his upper half on the edge of the sofa as Shane began to scramble backward, trying to get his bearings once more.

"What did you do?" the ghost bellowed, focusing on his maimed leg. Separated from the whole, the lower half had simply faded away like wisps of smoke in a breeze.

"I'm not done, don't worry," Shane answered. He slammed his fist down onto the side of Bolo's face.

Metal and ghostly flesh met. Still shocked that a living person could hurt him, the ghost stepped back a few feet away from Shane and toward the kitchen, giving Shane a chance to catch his breath.

He stood, a sharp pain rolling across his entire right side where he'd slammed against the wall. His reprieve only lasted seconds, however.

Bolo lifted the dining table and hurled it into the living room. Shane dropped to the floor, narrowly avoiding it before it crashed onto the floor.

Bolo fell to the ground and crawled like an animal, quickly covering the distance between himself and Shane. His huge hands, cold like ice, grasped for Shane's neck.

Under the ghost, Shane struggled to free himself and move the bigger man's arms. He bucked his hips and tried to flip the ghost.

"I'm going to watch your soul leave your body," Bolo hissed, leaning in close as he squeezed Shane's neck. They were nose to nose, and Shane writhed in the dead man's grip before opening his mouth and biting down on the ghost's face.

Bolo shrieked as Shane's teeth pierced ghostly flesh, tearing into it. It felt like biting a chunk of ice. He clamped his jaws shut and tore through the ghost's nose and upper lip, pulling them away in a strangely thick mouthful that immediately turned to nothingness. The ghost reeled back, grasping his own face.

Freed from the ghost's grip, Shane rolled immediately, giving himself the leverage and position as he climbed on top of Bolo.

Shane plunged his thumbs into the ghost's empty eye sockets, one on either side of the head, then bore down with all of his weight and strength, forcing his arms out as he did so.

Bolo's head popped like a melon that had been dropped, and then it broke apart. In an instant, Shane was launched backward, his back crunching into the busted dining table and TV as the entire building quaked from the shockwave.

Dust fell on Shane in thick, gritty bits as he lay on his back, staring up at the ceiling and breathing heavily. He felt like he'd just been hit by a car and knocked into a second car. He could taste blood in his mouth, and the room smelled of freshly kicked-up mold and old things.

Minutes passed, and he took the time to breathe and feel his pulse slowing down. Slowly, painfully, he rolled onto his side and looked around. The table and the sofa were in tatters, and there were cracks through the drywall and the ceiling as well.

Across the room, his phone had been pushed into a corner by the doorway to the bedroom. He got to his knees and spat blood on the floor, then took another moment to look around before getting up slowly and unsteadily.

He grunted once he was upright, then walked to the phone before leaning down and retrieving it. There was no doubt that it had been Jacinta who had called him. The ghost, Death's Head, had gotten to her, though.

He stared at the phone, and the screen switched before he could decide how he wanted to proceed. Jacinta's number popped up again. Shane inhaled sharply and pressed the button once more.

"Yeah?" he said.

"That's how you answer your phone?" came the reply. It was not Jacinta this time, but he did recognize the voice on the other end. Denise Sandoval.

"Sandoval?"

"You want to tell me what the hell is going on?" she demanded.

Shane looked around the apartment. Whatever she was talking about, it wasn't that.

"With what? Where's Jacinta?"

"She's on her way to Henry Ford Hospital. Looks like she called you, then ran right into a tree."

"Is she okay?"

"She drove into a tree. She's alive, if that's what you're asking. Paramedics said she's stable, probably with a concussion. What happened?"

"I'm not there, Sandoval, you tell me."

"She got up in the middle of interviewing one of the residents at this place we're investigating, left, called you, then crashed her car into a tree. Took ten minutes, tops. What did she talk to you about?"

"Nothing. Nothing important," he answered. That had to be another message from the ghost, just as Clem had been. He wondered if the ghost had intended to kill Jacinta and just failed to do so, or if this one was more of a warning. If Bolo was right, and Death's Head was looking to clean up the streets in some misguided superhero quest, then killing a cop would be out of character.

"You're going to stonewall me on this?" Sandoval said, anger tingeing her voice. Their relationship was tense at the best of times—due in no small part to the fact that Jacinta had to keep a lot of things about Shane's secret from her partner. Sandoval didn't know ghosts existed, and probably didn't want to know. For her, Shane was a recurring and untrustworthy nuisance.

Shane didn't think Sandoval doubted his sincerity as far as Jacinta was concerned. She'd seen him go to great lengths to keep her safe, and there was a kind of reluctant but mutual respect between them. But they were oil and water. Their worlds didn't mix, and he preferred it that way.

"If I had something to give you, I would. You want to grill me, you can do it in person. Just tell me what room she's in."

"She hasn't been checked in yet. Wait, when did you even arrive?" She sighed audibly. "Never mind, not my business. I'll meet you there."

Sandoval hung up. Shane slipped his phone back in his pocket and hobbled from the room. He had some time to try to think of a reasonable cover for what Jacinta might have called him about. As for being in town, it was just a visit. No need for Sandoval to know anything more than that. As far as she knew, the case they were working on had nothing to do with Shane and it would stay that way.

The kids were back when Shane crawled back out of the window. No one ran away this time as they watched him slowly drag himself out of the hole and get to his feet.

"Oh man, what happened in there?" Andre asked.

"Nothing," he replied.

"Nothing looks like it kicked your butt," the boy said.

"Nah. It tried to eat me, but I kicked its butt," he told the boy, and left them to finish their game.

✳

By the time Shane made it to the hospital, Jacinta had been admitted to a room on the fifth floor. He stopped in the lobby bathroom to clean himself up and make himself look at least partially decent. When Bolo had been destroyed, the explosion left small cuts across Shane's face and much of his body. But there was little to be done about it. He'd just tell people at the halfway house he had been in an accident at work.

Sandoval was seated in the room's lone chair when Shane arrived. Jacinta was asleep, her head bandaged, and a monitor hooked up to her beeped steadily.

"You look like hell," Sandoval told him as he entered the room. He let the dig slide. She wasn't wrong.

"How is she?"

"Concussion, broken ribs. Bruises. They said she'll be fine, though."

"Should she be asleep with a concussion?"

"Shouldn't you be in New Hampshire?"

"Came for a visit. Been staying out of your way, haven't I?"

They stared at each other for a moment, Sandoval's expression sour.

"Give me something, Ryan. Got a witness that said this wasn't an accident; she took a hard right into a tree. Timing matches up exactly with your phone call. One minute we're talking to some guy about a case; the next she gets up without a word, heads out to the car, and does this. Do you know anything at all that might help?"

"No. It doesn't make sense."

"Her phone log says she talked to you for just over a minute."

"Called to ask what I was doing. Made plans for later. It was nothing, really."

"One day, you're going to be honest with me, Ryan, and I'm sure I'm going to drop dead of a heart attack."

"I'm not as bad as you think, Sandoval. What were you doing before? Who were you interviewing?"

"Nothing that concerns you," the detective replied.

"Just saying, this halfway house thing has been taking up a lot of her time. She knew one of the guys who died, right?"

"Please don't be so obvious that you're fishing for information."

"She wasn't acting oddly before the interview, though, was she?"

"No, Shane, she wasn't. Wish you'd be as good at answering questions as you are at asking them."

He shrugged, looking back at Jacinta.

"If there was something I could tell you that would help you, I would," he said. "Listen, I'm not trying to get in the way. I'm just going to wait until she gets better, alright? You do your thing, I'll do mine."

"We'll see, huh? You know how to get in touch if your memory suddenly clears up," she said.

He chose to keep any further thoughts to himself and left the room to look for a doctor and get a better idea of Jacinta's injuries and how long she'd be unconscious.

Hurting Jacinta is going to be the biggest mistake of Death's Head's afterlife.

CHAPTER 16
THE SOURCE

Shane left the hospital and took a cab to Jacinta's, picking up his car from the driveway before he returned to the halfway house. He parked on the street next to the lot for the W4C employees behind the house, then walked around to the front of the building. It was earlier than it should have been, but the monitor at the door didn't question him signing back in. Abbott, however, caught him heading down the hall to the stairs and called out to him.

"You good?" the monitor asked.

"Yeah, everything's fine," he replied.

The other man checked his watch. "Couple of hours early for a full workday, isn't it?"

"Not as much to do as they thought, and I'm the low man on the totem pole, I guess."

"You look like you've been through hell."

Shane shrugged. "It's nothing. Just gravel kicked up by a truck. You know work sites."

"Alright," Abbot said. "You can get checked out by the doctor if you need to, though. Don't want you getting tetanus or something."

"I'm good. But I was thinking maybe I could talk to Price, if she's around."

"Mrs. Price? She's in, but she's booked solid. You can schedule an appointment, if you want."

"Yeah," Shane muttered. The rules of the house were really becoming a hindrance. Sandoval hadn't given him any info to go on, but Shane was certain the interview they were conducting had to have been at the house. And the ghost had a chance to get a hold of Jacinta, long enough to do what it had done.

Ghosts usually needed an in to possess someone. Depressed, suicidal, intoxicated, sick; the more vulnerable a person was, the easier they were to possess. Something that broke a person down physically or mentally could be used as an opening. But a strong ghost could take over a stronger person, someone with fewer vulnerabilities. At least long enough to make one call and steer a car into a tree.

"I haven't been assigned my chores for the week yet. Maybe I can do some work around here," Shane suggested. "Floors, windows, what's good?"

"You want to clean windows?" Abbott asked in disbelief.

He did not, but it would give him an excuse to be on any given floor by himself doing work no one paid attention to. "Good work. Needs to be done. Why not?"

Abbott shrugged. "Sure, alright. Let's get you hooked up."

Abbott took Shane to a supply room and showed him where everything he needed was located, then showed him how to log his work around the house. It was mundane and boring, but he needed to kill time.

He wasn't a hundred percent certain that Price was the person he was looking for, but she was still his best guess. If he couldn't get to her, he could keep tabs on her and see what she was up to. There had to be times when she was just herself. If the ghost was possessing other people, there had to be a reason she wasn't calling for help. The most obvious answer was that she was actually helping the ghost—or it was incapacitating her when it didn't need her.

Shane started with the windows on the second floor but only cleaned a few before heading up to the third floor where Price kept her office.

He tried to stay inconspicuous, spraying and wiping windows slowly and methodically, sometimes cleaning the same window several times. His hatred for undercover work was growing exponentially. It was going to be a cold day in hell before he volunteered for anything like it again.

Despite having an allegedly full schedule, he saw no one going into Price's office or coming out of it. Minutes became hours, and there was no sign anyone had even thought about coming to see her.

He wondered for a time if she was in the office at all, but shortly before dinnertime, the door at the end of the hall opened.

Shane slipped into an alcove by another office. Price left her office, locking the door behind her, and made her way toward the hallway and the stairs that led down. He waited a moment and made his way down the hall after her. In the stairwell, he listened to her slow and careful footfalls down the stairs, and then the opening of the door to the first floor.

He followed her quickly, then made his way through the building, searching for her. He caught up with her at the entrance as she signed out for the night, exchanging pleasantries with the door monitor.

Shane doubled back the way he had come, heading to the yard in the rear of the house. Several other residents were there, reading or playing games. It would do little to help his cover at that moment, but he didn't have many choices. And he'd been looking forward to breaking his own cover for a while, anyway.

He walked across the yard to the back fence and the wall of fir trees that mostly obscured it, pushing aside some of the growth to peer out to the world beyond. He had a good view of the parking lot and waited until Price appeared.

Price drove a compact sedan, a car that suited her to a T. As she pulled out of the lot, Shane made his move. Someone called out behind him, but he paid them no mind as he braced one foot on a small fir tree and pulled himself quickly up and over the fence. The honor system was a good way to keep people on the property when they truly did want to stay there, but not having serious fences made it easy enough to get out.

He landed in the parking lot and ran across to the street and his own car. He reached the road just in time to see Price take a left at the corner.

Shane got into his car and followed the woman, nearly clipping a city bus to get ahead of it. He pursued her down the street, weaving past a handful of vehicles until he caught sight of her small car once again. He followed at a safe distance for several minutes as she made her way across town.

Price led him into a quiet residential neighborhood in one of the nicer parts of Detroit. The streets were tree-lined and sleepy, and traffic was minimal. Shane held back as far as he could while keeping the car in sight, and watched as Price finally signaled and pulled off the road into the driveway of a ranch-style yellow brick house set back from the road behind a big, empty lawn and hidden behind a handful of shrubs.

Shane rolled to a stop as close as he dared while Price got out of her car and made her way to the front door of the house. With keys in hand, she checked the mailbox, reaching inside for a moment, then unlocked the door before entering the house.

Shane waited for five minutes. There was no movement from the house that he could see, no indication Price was on the way back out. He got out of his car and made his way casually across the street.

He pondered simply knocking on the door, confronting Price directly, but wasn't convinced it was his best option. He'd already gone toe-to-toe with a ghost once that day; he didn't want to do it again. This time, he wanted to be holding some cards.

Shane walked up the driveway toward the house. Then, rather than following the small cobblestone path to the front door, he continued down the side of the house to the backyard, passing through a gate and onto a rear patio.

He crouched low next to a large window and peered inside through vertical blinds that had been left open. The interior showed a living room: neat and empty. There was no sign of Price or anyone else.

The next window looked into the kitchen, and there too, Shane saw nothing that looked suspicious or out of the ordinary, and there was no sign of the woman.

The backdoor was made of glass and gave a clear look across most of the floor. The house appeared empty. Wherever she had gone was deeper in the house, somewhere out of sight.

Shane tried the doorknob. It turned easily, and the door fell open.

The house smelled stale. It looked like it would have a potpourri odor about it, like a grandmother's house. Instead, it smelled musty, like clothes that had been in a closet for too long. He moved silently into the kitchen and opened the door to the refrigerator. There was little inside, but some of it was clearly old, grown over with mold inside Tupperware containers.

Closing the refrigerator, Shane made his way down the adjoining hallway. A door on his right was open, and like the other rooms, the bedroom looked the part, but had an unused quality to it. The bed was made, the carpet was clean and bare. The walls were decorated with art and photos that all seemed appropriate for an older woman. But there was a distinct layer of dust on them as well. No one had been in the bedroom for some time.

He continued deeper into the house. To the right of the front door was what looked like a closet with the door slightly ajar. Inside, a set of stairs headed down into the basement, where a light was still on.

With one last look around the main floor, Shane headed down the steps to the floor below. The stairs were well-made, and his feet didn't make a sound as he made his way down. The air was cooler in the basement, thanks to the concrete walls and floor.

The space fit with everything he had seen upstairs. Neatly packed plastic totes on shelves labeled with tags like "Christmas" and "Garden". It was the basement of an organized old woman. But just like upstairs, dust had built up. Not like at Pop Shop, but enough to suggest no one had tried to clean it in months.

Most of the basement had an open layout. A work bench and some tools were on one wall, and shelves held more totes. There was a washer and dryer next to a laundry tub and a stand-up freezer as well. Next to the freezer, however, was another door.

Shane approached the door cautiously, keeping an eye out for anything else that might have been hiding in the corners of the basement. Nothing moved, however. No sounds or even gusts of cool air burst out to surprise him.

The knob had a simple lock on it from Shane's side. It meant someone inside would need a key to get out.

Shane turned the knob to unlock the door, and he pushed it slowly and carefully, his eyes scanning the room within. It was not dark as he'd been expecting, with light coming from a small desk lamp on the far side of the room.

Jocelyn Price was chained to a bed on the far side of the room against a wall. Her wrists and ankles were shackled. It looked like she had enough slack to move a small distance, judging by both the length of the chains and the plate of food and bottle of water sitting on a small table a few feet away.

The woman was unconscious, and whoever had chained her had likely been doing it for some time, as the chains were anchored into the cement of the floor under the bed. The room had been set up to keep someone captive.

With no windows and no means of escape, Price would not have been able to get any help when she woke up. The ghost kept her alive by providing food, and no one ever would have suspected there was a problem, since they saw her coming and going regularly. Only it wasn't Price at all. It was someone capable of controlling a living human.

It's got to be Death's Head.

The muffled sound of a car door closing drew Shane's attention. The only car nearby was Price's in the driveway out front.

He rushed back up the stairs to the front door. Price's car was at the end of the driveway, pulling out onto the street. From the window, Shane couldn't make out the face of the driver. Shane realized the ghost was keeping two people in the house, alternating between them. It was either to throw off suspicion, or just to keep them both running and healthy. He let one sleep while he used the other.

A realization suddenly dawned on Shane.

His opponent was strategic just as it was cruel.

CHAPTER 17
AND BACK AGAIN

Shane rushed out of the house to his own car as Price's vanished down the street. His wheels squealed as he made a sharp turn on the road to give chase. He caught up to the small car once more just a few blocks up. The ghost was retracing the path it had taken to get to Price's house. Shane was certain that the ghost was returning to the halfway house.

It was only in the final minutes that the journey took an alternate course. Rather than turning down the road toward the W4C building parking lot, Price's car continued another block, then turned.

Another block up, and Price's car came to a stop across the street from the Pop Shop. A man got out of Price's car—younger than her, but likely in his fifties from the looks of things. He was average height and a little paunchy, with graying, slicked-back hair and a weathered face. Shane had never seen him before.

The man crossed the street to the boarded-up store and made his way around the back. Shane waited a moment before getting out of his car and following the man.

There was no sign of the man at the back of the building. Like Shane earlier that day, he had gone in through the window.

Shane stared at the building. It was his best opportunity to find out who and what he was dealing with.

I hope this isn't a trap. He got to his knees and slipped in through the window.

He heard the wood floor above him creak as someone made their way up the topmost floor. Shane moved quickly, keeping to one side of the basement stairs so they'd creak less as he climbed them.

The footsteps allowed him to guess where the man was upstairs—the kitchen area, from the sounds of the things. He heard a voice call out for Bolo a few seconds after.

"He's not going to answer you," Shane said, stepping around the corner to confront the man.

The stranger stood still, locking eyes with Shane. The corners of his mouth curved into a smile. "I guess I shouldn't be surprised."

"No?"

"If anyone was going to put Bolo down, it was you, right? That seems to be your thing."

"I didn't know I had a thing."

"Oh, don't be modest. You're the… ghost fighter? Ghost hunter? I don't know if you have an official title for what you do."

"I don't." Shane rolled his eyes.

"You should consider it. Would look good on a business card, probably."

"I'll keep that in mind."

The man chuckled and nodded, leaning against the kitchen counter.

"Yeah. I was hoping for something—maybe a miracle? I don't know. I figured if anyone had a chance, it'd be Bolo. A big ghost has to be tougher than a small ghost. At least that's what I thought."

"That's not really how it works."

"No? There has to be something, right?"

"Age, usually," Shane offered. "Not how old a ghost was when they died, more like, how long they've been dead. Just like everything else, experience is the key."

"Makes sense," the man nodded again. "So, how old are we talking about here? Like fifty years, or five hundred years? How old can a ghost get?"

"No limit, as far as I know. Older than you, that's for sure. You're real new, huh?"

"If ghosts can live forever, then I guess I must be."

"Who is he?"

"What, this sack I'm wearing? He's Dayton," the man replied. "Tom Dayton."

"The former administrator," Shane said.

Dayton smiled. "Heard that story, huh? Useless idiot. Got caught up in drugs, then got fired. Kind of put a speed bump on the road for me."

"So you switched to Jocelyn Price."

"Well, I had to. Had to shake it up. I was only part-timing Dayton here before. He'd get high, I'd take over; he'd think he just blacked out. But I gave him too much freedom. Now, I got two of them. When one needs to rest, I lock them up and use the other. Just like you said, experience is the key. I learned from experience, so I adapted." He chuckled at his own joke.

Now that Shane had him cornered, he couldn't place who the ghost inside could have been. No one with any discernible tells. Who the hell in Detroit would have known who he was and what he did?

"So, I've been made from the start, then, huh?"

"This little undercover thing you're doing? Oh, yes. I knew you'd get involved even before I saw you, really. The moment I saw Detective Perez, I assumed you'd be nearby."

"And you tried to kill her."

"No," Dayton scoffed. "If I wanted to kill her, you'd be picking pieces of her off of Woodward Avenue now. I just gave her a scare. Or you, really."

"Got my attention, that's for sure."

"That was the plan."

"Well, things are mostly going your way, it seems," Shane said. "Are we going to keep playing games, or are you going to tell me who you are?"

Dayton grinned and shrugged playfully.

"You're not even going to try guessing? You seem like a smart guy. How many ghosts do you meet in your line of work, anyway? More than you can keep track of?"

"You'd be surprised," Shane answered.

"Maybe I would be. I was surprised when this all started, I can tell you that. I was surprised when it all just kept going. It kept going, and people kept doing things, and no one did anything about it. Not Perez and her partner. Sure as hell not you. No one did a damn thing."

"I have no idea what you're talking about."

Dayton snorted. "Of course not. End of the world for me. For you? Something you can't even remember. Like it was nothing."

"Enlighten me, then."

Dayton stood up straight and held his arms out. He then collapsed onto the floor in a heap, but something remained in his place. The ghost stayed where the living man had been. The spirit was shorter than Dayton, and his face was just what the others had described.

The ghost had the head of a man, but his flesh was split with fine, spider web-like cuts and slices across the forehead, and where eyes and a nose should have been.

Only a mouth marred the relatively smooth surface, a too-big swatch of red grinning teeth. A skeleton's mouth—red and raw, like someone had just pulled the lips off of his face. There was no blood, but it was still wet and raw.

The effect was too much like the bandanas that Hawthorn had worn. But without a true face, Shane still had no clue what he was seeing.

"You don't recognize me, do you?" the ghost asked.

Shane's eyes narrowed. There was something there, something in the voice.

"No," he answered honestly. The skeletal face twitched, muscles moving below the surface creating an expression Shane had never seen before. The face made no sense to him. He'd seen ghosts that had died in brutal ways, but none that had a new face when they became a ghost. The only thing even close to this ghost that he could think of was Machine Man, the ghost of a man who had been killed in an industrial machine accident. His body had been so badly damaged that his ghost didn't even look human.

"You are such a liar, did you know that?"

"I really don't know who you are."

"Not that. Who cares if you remember me? You're a liar because of what you tell people. Pretending to help people. Saving the day? What an absolute joke."

Shane rolled his eyes and sighed. "Stop with the riddles already, will you? I have better things to do."

"When I still had a face, you lied to it. You made me think you'd help me. You told me you'd be able to get rid of Hawthorn and destroy him, then I'd be okay. I'd get to be like that girl, and get away. I'd be a survivor. But that didn't happen, did it?"

The voice clicked in Shane's head. Chris Jessop.

"Is that it?" the ghost said, pointing at Shane's face. "Is that your look of recognition?"

"Jessop," Shane said.

The red, angry mouth spread into a cruel mockery of a smile.

Hawthorn had possessed Jessop back in Canada. A member of the crime scene cleanup crew, Jessop had been taking care of the mess left in the aftermath of Hawthorn's death. But the ghost had latched on and taken him to Detroit in pursuit of Jacinta. And while Jessop, he had continued his bloody killing spree, until Shane finally destroyed him.

Hawthorn had been outside of Jessop when Shane destroyed him, but his haunted item, a skull-mouth bandana, had been inside Jessop's guts. When he was possessed, Hawthorn must have made the man eat the bandana. It ensured that the ghost would always be able to travel within a mile of Jessop himself.

But destroying Hawthorn had caused the bandana to explode inside Jessop, killing him as well. Shane hadn't meant to do it—and wouldn't have done it if he'd known.

"Guess that explains your face. Kind of exploded when you died."

"See? My life and my death never meant anything to you. You're like the rest of the monsters that I'm trying to rid the world of. You're just a killer."

"Your death was an accident," Shane reminded him. "We were trying to save you and a lot of other people."

"Of course you were. Is that what you tell yourself to help you sleep at night?"

"You could have told me the guy made you eat his bandana," Shane pointed out.

The flesh around the skeleton mouth twitched and pulled back into a snarl. "I didn't know!"

Shane shrugged. "So, you didn't know, and I was supposed to? You had that guy in your head. If you had the chance to kill him, would you have hesitated?"

"I didn't have a chance. You did. And this was the best you could do. You killed me. I was innocent!"

Shane waited for more, but Jessop didn't say anything else. "Oh, is that it? You done?"

Jessop's lips curled back, and Shane shrugged.

"Like I said, I didn't mean to kill you. I'm sorry you died, if that's what you want to hear. It was an accident, alright? Hawthorn needed to be stopped, so I stopped him first chance I got. Had I known you'd be killed in the process, I would have waited and come up with a different plan."

"Yeah, you destroyed him, like you're some self-appointed executioner."

Shane snorted, half at Jessop's misplaced anger and half at the indignant tone. "And you're not? All this killing the criminals doesn't make you a self-appointed executioner? Yeah, your clean up the streets act. Bolo told me about it. Before I busted his head open like a coconut."

"Maybe you're just too crass to understand." Jessop shook his head. "I always wanted to make a difference, you know? Wasn't fit to be a cop; couldn't pass the exams. But I tried to help. And cleaning up crime scenes was helping. But this? This is something else. I can do so much more like this than I ever could before. And I can help people for real, not like you. Not with careless disregard."

"Just a true superhero, you are."

"I am a good person. I can stop what happened to me from happening to others."

"By making guys like Clem overdose?"

"He was a criminal. He was in a gang. People like him don't change. They don't get out of prison and become upstanding citizens. They just go right back to what they know. Robbing, carjacking, drug dealing, murdering. I'm saving everyone the trouble of dealing with them."

"So you'll kill all prisoners and felons?" Shane asked.

"I'll kill the bad ones to save the good."

"As judged by you. Again, self-appointed executioner."

"Come on, you don't believe any of these people are good. And even if you do, so what? They can consider it 'life's last great injustice'," Jessop countered.

Shane needed to get close enough to Jessop to put an end to him. Jessop was not going to fight. He knew what Shane could do. He'd avoid confrontation. Which meant Shane needed to close the gap and take him by surprise.

"How about the lives of two innocent people?"

"Two people?" Jessop asked.

Shane nodded to the floor. "Him and Price."

"This idiot is a drug trafficker. He needed to finance his growing addiction and used his position to let the residents under his care deal drugs. He's not exactly innocent. But he and Price are clean in this. The people I take out kill themselves. Price doesn't kill them. He doesn't kill them. I'm not ruining their lives."

"Man, you'd thought of everything, huh?"

"I had. Then you showed up, so I have to make a small change to my plans."

"Yeah, yeah, whatever. I'll give it to you, Jessop, you are wildly creative in your afterlife. This is next-level crap you're shoveling."

"Enjoy it while you can, Shane. Your time is up."

CHAPTER 18
KING BADGER

A rush of cold air was the only warning. Pain tore through Shane's back as something sharp and cold sliced him from the neck to his waist. He collapsed to his knees, shocked by the sudden blow that had split him open.

He could feel blood, hot against the cold of the wound, running down his sides as he fell to his hands and knees.

A fist, cold and hard as rock, crushed against the side of his face. A second blow followed, and then more. Fists rained down on him. Shane struggled to protect himself and defend, but a tall, muscular ghost peppered with gunshot wounds on the chest did not waver in his assault.

"Badger here was Bolo's brother," Jessop said. He was back inside Dayton's body and standing on the other side of the kitchen watching the new ghost attack Shane. "He's not too happy about what you did to his brother, as I can imagine."

Another icy claw dug into Shane's side, and he bit back a yell of pain. He scrambled and kicked, his foot hitting something, giving him enough time to regain his footing.

Badger attacked again, and now Shane could see another wound dead center in the ghost's head, where someone had shot him almost between the eyes. The ghost took wild swings and hit like his hands were made of lead. Shane blocked as well as he could while looking for ins to fight back.

"They used to call him King Badger. He was an amateur

boxer," Dayton explained. "He was good, too, as you can see. Those long arms of his. Hard to find an opening, isn't it?"

Shane said nothing as he was busy protecting himself from the ghost's furious blows. He knew how to fight; Dayton wasn't wrong about that. He switched high to low and back, looking for openings in Shane's defense.

With two serious cuts on his back and side, Shane knew he needed to end the fight quickly, but Badger was not likely to be compliant. His only thought was to at least make it to the paper-covered window and get outside.

Shane took a step towards the window, plotting the best way to escape, when something heavy crashed against the back of his head. In his haste to keep track of Badger, he had forgotten to pay attention to Dayton.

His vision swam black, and his legs went weak beneath him. He didn't feel his own body hit the floor.

✳

That cold, moldy, earthy smell filled Shane's nose as his eyes came open with a start. Cold metal at his wrists held him in place. Someone had chained him up, the same way Price had been restrained in her home.

He jerked his arms, but the chain held fast. The rattle of the metal filled the space, and a quiet laugh answered. He followed the sound with his eyes and saw Dayton leaning against one of the rusted metal shelves.

"That was so much easier than I expected," the man said, grinning.

Shane focused his attention on the chains again, looking to see if there was any weak point in how they'd been fastened to him.

"I get it, Shane. I understand the frustration. You're not technically a bad person. You don't go out there looking to murder people. You're not Hawthorn. But at the end of the day, if the things you do get people killed, does it matter if you did it on purpose or by accident?"

"Not to you, obviously," Shane muttered, straining against the chains.

"No, not to me."

"So I can see," Shane said. The chains were too tight to escape without a lot of work, he was sure. He needed either more time, or something to help work himself loose, neither of which he'd accomplish with Dayton looming over him.

"My work here is making the world better. Safer. And in that world, you are just as evil as the rest of the criminals in that halfway house. Just as bad as Hawthorn. Because you're a liability, I can't let you go. I hope you understand that."

"Do you?" Shane asked.

Dayton shrugged. "I do. It doesn't matter, I guess. I'm just trying to make you see where I stand."

"I see it just fine. I'm not really seeing a lot of difference, is all. You'll kill criminals. You'll kill me. You'll crash a cop into a tree. I don't need you to justify things, I honestly don't care. But it seems like you do, and your justification is about as busted as your face."

"Hmm," Jessop said. "We can talk all day like this, just going in circles. But we don't have to, because you're chained up and I'm not. That means I win."

"What's the prize for winning? You get to throw me off the roof? Pump me full of pills?" Shane asked.

Dayton shook his head. "Of course not. I'm going to leave you here."

"In the basement?"

"In the basement. In chains. All by yourself. Have you ever seen someone die of dehydration? It's cool down here, and dark and damp. You might last four days if you're lucky. Or unlucky; I'm not sure which word is best in this case. But that's my gift to you. Time. Time to sit here and think about what you could have done differently. And who knows? Maybe you'll get to come back, and we can talk about it later."

"Hell of a plan."

Dayton shrugged again. "Came up with it on the fly. Enjoy your slow death, Shane."

"Why not kill him now?" another voice asked suddenly. Badger was in the basement with them as well. He had been hiding in the shadows. Now he came forward, eyes locked on Shane.

"I just explained why," Dayton answered.

Badger sneered. "After what he did to you? Then my brother? He's worse than the criminals we've killed so far. He deserves nothing but pain."

"You don't think this will be painful? This is torture. Mental and physical. Knowing he failed. Knowing he's dying. Feeling helpless. Feeling his body shutting down as it sucks every last drop from his organs to try to stay alive. He'll know pain. Trust me."

"It's not fair! He—"

"It is fair," Dayton interrupted. "Bolo and Shane fought. Bolo lost. You were a fighter in life; did you ever get revenge when you lost an even fight? Ever complained that it wasn't just? That's being a sore loser."

"'Fair' fight," Badger corrected, practically hissing.

"You should remember your brother as the man he was. That he got to come back and atone for his mistakes in life. Remember how he tried to make this place better for everyone. To make your neighborhood better. That's what we need to focus on."

Badger grunted, fixing Shane with a vengeful stare, and Dayton snapped his fingers in Badger's face until he had his attention.

"He's dead no matter what. Let him die. We have other, more important things to do."

Dayton didn't wait for a response and just crawled out of the back window to leave, while Badger simply vanished, leaving Shane alone in the basement.

The wounds on his back and side burned. The chains binding him had been looped around and under each other and padlocked in place. He'd have to work the lock if he wanted to escape; slipping out didn't seem like an option.

He stood up and checked the slack on the chain. He'd been given some, but not much. He could walk a few paces, and no more. There was nothing within range that looked like it might make a useful tool for freeing himself, either. Mostly trash, bits of wood and plastic and cardboard. Towards the furthest corner of the basement, just beyond his reach, was a misshapen mound. He crouched low, getting as close as he could, and reached for the piece of dirty old fabric covering the unusual shape. He could just barely grasp it with his fingertips, and slowly eased it back until he had a firm enough grip to pull it fully.

Beneath it was a pile of bodies.

There were four that Shane could make out, long since dead, covered in papery old flesh. One of them bore serious gouges in the skull over the eyes, as though a large blade had been stabbed into them. Bolo, Shane thought. The bodies of Bolo and his family.

He sat on the floor and looked at the remains. Murdered in their home, based on what Bolo had told him. But the bodies were still there. No one had come for them. No one had investigated. Or not well, anyway.

Dayton had removed anything Shane had carried in his pockets. He was stuck in the basement, and his options seemed to be growing more limited by the moment.

The movement of light in the window marked the passage of time. He passed the time working the chain, link after link, looking for any weakness he could find and coming up with nothing.

The ghost had even taken his cigarettes. It was not the way he had envisioned himself going out. The only person who was likely to really go looking for him was Jacinta, and as far as he knew, she was still unconscious.

The halfway house would likely have done something, called the police or the Department of Corrections. But if it got back to Lo Truglio, he'd likely make it go away. Or maybe Price would cover it up. Odds were, no one was going to stumble into the Pop Shop or Jocelyn Price's place looking for Shane Ryan.

Eventually, Shane decided it would be best to conserve his energy. He could start again in the morning, and see if he could dig up a tool somewhere. If there was a way to get out, he'd find it.

And then he'd make sure Jessop regretted not killing him when he had the chance.

CHAPTER 19
A WAY

The kick hit Shane square in the gut. He coughed as his body curled instinctively, waking him from a fitful sleep. The basement was still dark and cold, no sign of light peeking through the broken window, and no way to know how long he'd been sleeping or what time it was.

"Wake up," Badger's voice said over him. Shane grunted awkwardly and forced himself up to a sitting position. The ghost had come back without Jessop.

"Figured I'd see you again," Shane said.

"I could have killed you in your sleep."

Shane shrugged. "Could have. But didn't."

"I didn't. Because I wanted you to know it was me. I wanted your last memory to be this. So you regret what you've done to Bolo."

"That guy?" Shane asked, pointing across the room at the pile of bodies. Badger looked back. Shane couldn't see the ghost's face in the darkness, but he didn't move for a long moment.

"You shouldn't have disturbed them," he said, more quietly than a moment earlier.

"Didn't know they were there. But that's him, isn't it? They stabbed his eyes out."

"Yeah, they did," Badger confirmed. "They didn't make empty threats."

"Got in deep with someone?"

"Doesn't matter," Badger said. "None of your business, anyway."

"Just saying," Shane said. "Looks like dealing with the wrong people got your whole family killed once. Now you're putting your trust in someone else who's using you."

"Like you'd know."

"I know manipulation when I see it."

Badger leaned down and punched Shane in the face, then punched him again. Shane's vision swam, and lights flashed in his eyes. He tried to shake it off as Badger held back from another blow.

"You talk too much," the ghost said.

Shane laughed, spitting out blood. "Most people would disagree."

"Most people aren't going to kill you."

Shane chuckled and spat once more. "Ahh. Well, if you put it that way. Still won't change the fact you're just being used by a ghost who thinks he's some vigilante hero."

Badger grunted, crouching down to face him. "You don't know what it's like to be in a place like this when everything begins to go to hell. This whole city died. The money vanished. People fled like rats, and all that was left was the garbage and the people who couldn't leave. Or wouldn't. My parents thought things would turn around. You see what that got them."

He pointed to the dead bodies. Shane understood what the ghost was saying but couldn't understand why it was so easy for him to fall for Jessop's crusade.

"Lots of people had a bad turn around here," Shane said.

Badger growled. "Bad turn? They were shot. Because of me. Because of the people I ran with, the people I crossed. I was supposed to look after Bolo out on the streets. He looked big, but he was an idiot. I was the big brother. I was a tough guy. I was supposed to watch his back. And when he rolled on the Red Kings after seeing what they did up in Fiskhorn, they took his eyes! They shot Mom and Pop, and plugged me when I got home, too. So that's our bad turn, huh? That's just how the world works?"

"Never said it was good or right," Shane pointed out.

Badger scoffed, shaking his head. "You know what happened after? The cops came, searched upstairs for maybe ten minutes. Me and Bolo, we had rap sheets. It was a gang hit; they knew it. They never even came down here. Never even looked for our bodies. They let my family rot down here where they were dumped, and no one cared. So yeah, man. I listen to Jessop. To the guy who wants to make sure people care what goes on around here. Someone who has the power to make it happen, and who no one can stop."

"Wow," Shane said quietly. "Must be rough being the only person in the world who has bad luck. You should write a book."

The ghost's jaw tensed, and his teeth clenched. Shane did nothing and simply waited. If he was going to die chained in a basement, he didn't plan to listen to anyone's sob story along the way.

Ghosts often had a bad case of main character syndrome, and this wasn't the first time Shane had encountered it. There was a tendency to focus on whatever mistakes, injustices, or perceived slights they'd endured in life.

On the one hand, it made sense. A soul that returned was rarely the same as the one that left. Many came back different, to a greater or lesser degree. Some came back better that who they had been in life. Most didn't, though. Their impulses, their anger, their rationality—all of it had suffered in the transition. The result left them focusing too intently on themselves and their own issues.

On the other hand, Shane just didn't care. It was not much different from a fully living narcissist. Someone who couldn't relate to anything in the world without filtering it through the prism of their own self-interest. Bolo and Badger may have had an unfair shake in life, but so did a million people each and every day.

The worst part of it all was the way they couldn't move on. They never moved on. Spiritual growth from a spirit? Not so much. And that led to things like Shane being chained in a basement, listening to another sad-sack tale of injustice and a life unfulfilled. It was enough to make him wish the ghost would at least try to beat him to death so they could get to the end of the story faster.

"Jessop was right about you. You're a goddamn piece of trash," Badger said with a sneer.

Shane grinned. "Did he ever explain to you how he died? He exploded. Fully exploded. Because I had to stop a killer that had possessed him. He's just got a chip on his shoulder. He's not mad at me; he's mad at himself that he couldn't live out his hero fantasy when he was alive. A killer used him, made him kill, and all he could do was watch."

"That makes you a better man?" Badger asked.

Shane shrugged. "I don't need to be better. Just saying I'm not the reason you've lost your brother again. That's on him."

Badger's eyes narrowed. The blood flowing from the bullet wound in his forehead trickled and dripped down his nose.

"You destroyed Bolo," he said, but there was a faint hint of a question behind it.

"I did. Because Jessop set him up to die. He knew my face the moment I walked into that halfway house. He knew I was here, talking to your brother. He possessed my girlfriend to call me on the phone and then asked to talk to Bolo. He told him to kill me, knowing Bolo wasn't a fighter and that I could very well destroy him. He figured it was worth a shot. Maybe your brother kills me. If not, no big loss. Because Jessop doesn't give a damn about you any more than I do. He'd sacrifice your brother, he'd sacrifice you, he'd sacrifice anyone. He's full of crap."

The ghost stared at him, and Shane could see the range of emotions crossing his face. He was conflicted, and he didn't want to believe Shane, but he must have known that parts of it had to be true. Jessop knew who Shane was. And he knew what Shane could do to a ghost. The pieces fit together.

"It doesn't change anything for you," Badger said. "If Jessop set up my brother, then I'll make sure he gets what's coming to him. But you're the one who did it. You're the one who destroyed him."

Shane leaned in conspiratorially. "So, what are you going to do about it?"

CHAPTER 20
TIGHTENING THE NOOSE

Shane knew ghosts were very often fueled by emotion. Some could overcome that, and even control it. But others would lose themselves in it. Badger was one of those.

The act of dying was clearly not good for anyone's mind. Many ghosts were consumed by rage, hate, and other negative feelings. And even those that could mostly keep it in check found themselves teetering on the edge when provoked.

Shane had not spent enough time with Badger to get a solid read on who he was or and how his thought process worked. But it seemed clear enough that he let his emotions take the lead in his decisions. He was fueled by passion, rage included, and that meant he wasn't always thinking. It was not hard for Shane to push Badger over that edge.

The ghost's expression twisted with pure anger, and he lunged at Shane with murder in his dead eyes.

The chains binding Shane rattled as he scrambled backward, forcing the ghost to chase him to the corner. With the way his wrists were bound, he was only to separate his hands about six or seven inches, while the rest of the chain kept him on a tether limiting where and how he could maneuver around the spirit. It was not going to be an easy fight. But it was better than starving to death in a basement.

Badger came at Shane with clenched fists. He swung and missed, then lashed out again, open-handed this time, using his fingers like claws the way he had when he sliced Shane's back open.

The ghost fought like a boxer, just as Shane had hoped. His anger was clouding his judgment, and he likely had fought little as a ghost. Or had not been dead long enough to comprehend the differences. Not understanding his own strengths was something exploitable.

Shane dodged left, extending his chain to its full length, and drawing the ghost closer. Badger missed with another wild punch. He was following rules, fighting like a boxer who expected his opponent to be standing and using time-honored regulation moves to block, parry and attack.

Shane balled both hands into fists and brought them up together under the ghost's chin, slamming his mouth shut and forcing his head to snap back. Had he been a living man, the blow probably would have cracked a tooth or two. Being dead, it definitely stunned him for at least a moment.

Badger stumbled back, putting a hand to his jaw as his eyes narrowed. The blow was a surprise, but it did give the spirit time to rethink his approach.

"He said you could do that. You could hurt us," the ghost said.

"He was right."

"Is that what you did to my brother?"

"Oh. No, I just tore his head open."

Badger grunted and reached down. He grabbed hold of the chain that anchored Shane in place and pulled it. The action caught Shane off guard, falling face-first with his arms extended.

The ghost was on Shane's back immediately. The pressure on Shane's spine made him grunt, and the first blow to the side of his head stunned him to silence.

"What do you think will happen when I break your head open?" Badger asked, slamming another fist into Shane's temple. "Think any more of your jokes will slip out?"

Badger continued punching hammer-like blows to the right side of

Shane's head. With a growl of frustration, Shane gripped the chain tether and wrapped his right hand up in it. He used the chain for stability as he pulled and rolled at the same time.

Badger lurched to one side as Shane put all his effort into moving his body, bracing himself with the chain and kicking off with his feet as he forced the ghost over. Badger was caught off-guard—and it was all the break Shane had needed.

The ghost fell to the side. He tried to speak but was cut short as Shane's foot met his mouth. This time, teeth did come free, ghostly fragments that shattered under the force of Shane's boot crashing into his jaw.

He kicked out again, aiming lower this time, and clipping the spirit in the chin instead.

Badger fell back, a cry of rage escaping his busted mouth. Shane found his footing long enough to put his own weight on the spirit.

As a boxer, Badger had been used to fighting on his feet. Lying on his side and against an opponent who knew no rules, he was not prepared. Even as he pulled his hands away from his mouth, Shane was on top of him. Chained hands looped over the ghost's head as Shane fell to the ground.

The chain stretched as far as it could, and as far as Shane needed it to. He tightened his hold so the chain links stayed lodged between Badger's broken lips as he tried to grip the sides of the spirit's head.

The fit was tight and awkward, and Shane had none of the leverage he wanted, but he wasn't looking for finesse. He needed to get the job done, nothing more.

He dug his knees in harder against Badger's ribs and pulled back with his arms. Locking the ghost into his grip, he forced the ghostly body to bend in unnatural ways.

Badger cried out, a muffled sound of rage and desperation. The chain pressed into his mouth, and Shane's hands were strained on the sides of his face.

Shane took in a deep breath and held it, using all of his remaining strength to push with his knees and pull with his arms. Teeth gritted, a growl erupted low in his throat as the pain in his wrists came close to unbearable. One or the other would have to give—either his body or the ghost's.

Badger's head shuddered, and suddenly, Shane felt himself jerk back further, with more room to move. The chain broke the ghost's jaw and allowed Shane to shift his weight, pressing in now instead of pulling back. The ghost roared wordless and bestial screams, until his head collapsed under Shane.

Badger's body burst like a melon. Torn from whatever power fueled the existence of a soul beyond death, the force of the spirit-energy exploded into Shane like a bomb. The chain at his wrists shattered, links flying apart as he was tossed backwards like a ragdoll. He landed roughly, the wind knocked out of him, but with a smile on his face despite the immense pain.

Shane rolled onto his back, staring up in the darkness. He breathed deeply, the smell of the old, stale air filling his nose. After a few minutes, the pain he felt had lessened.

He clumsily pulled the loosely looped remains of the chains from his wrists, and groaned as he sat up. His body ached from previously destroying Bolo. The added stress of taking out his brother so soon after felt like a full-body, deep-tissue bruise. He needed a real night's sleep—in something other than a stale dungeon. A cup of coffee wouldn't hurt, either.

In the dark, he sat still and took deep, calming breaths as he checked to make sure nothing was broken or missing. He was beaten, but nothing so badly damaged that he wouldn't heal. The pressure had cut into his wrists so badly, he could still make out the shape of the chain links in red and blue and purple in his skin, but his wrists still worked.

He had a slight advantage of time, he realized, slowly getting to his feet. Jessop was not aware that Badger had come back to kill him. That meant Jessop assumed he was still free of Shane, and would remain so. Even if he did come back to make sure Shane was dead, it probably wouldn't be for a couple of days.

Shane needed to pace himself, work out some kind of plan. He needed to get Jessop outside of whatever body he was possessing—whether that be Price or Dayton or someone else. And he needed to check on Jacinta. He was really beginning to lose patience with this ghost.

Jessop was proving to be more aggravating to Shane than even Hawthorn had. At least he understood who and what Hawthorn was. Hawthorn was evil and twisted, but that was easy to see and understand. He was a killer, and even if he hid behind the badge of a cop when he was alive, it was clear as day once he was exposed. Shane understood how to deal with that.

Jessop was a bird of a different feather. He had not been anyone significant in life, as far as Shane knew. He was the same as a million other people—just a normal guy with a normal job. His death—specifically, the events leading up to it and the manner in which it happened—had turned him into something else.

His attitude in death reminded Shane of an arrogant and entitled person who assumed the world owed them something. The kind of person who felt their own hardships made them more special than everyone else, and more deserving of special praise and consideration. The kind of person who refused to look at the bigger picture because it took the focus off themselves.

It wasn't rare, Shane recognized. Dying literally and figuratively removed someone from the world, from life. Those that came back didn't see the big picture because they didn't want to—and in a lot of ways, they just couldn't. Relating to the world was hard when you were no longer of the world.

That meant Jessop's misplaced sense of entitlement was going to fester, because it was one of the only things he had left. He'd been wronged, and he was writing his own heroic story of how he'd right those wrongs.

All of that would need to be dealt with later, Shane knew. But first, he needed to leave the basement and see Jacinta. Or at least contact her.

Shane awkwardly made his way to the basement window and crawled painfully into the yard outside the Pop Shop, taking another long moment in the weeds behind the building to catch his breath.

If Shane had to guess, he would assume Jessop was going to proceed as planned. As far as he was concerned, Shane had been dealt with. He might be forced to do something once Jacinta came looking, but even then, she wouldn't risk doing or saying anything. No one would believe her, and Jessop knew that.

With the ghost sticking to his plans, it meant he'd be keeping his focus on the halfway house. No matter how many residents died there, no authority would ever be able to concretely link them to Price or anyone living. And even if they tried, it would only jam up those people Jessop had used. The ghost would just move to someone else and keep his little quest going forward.

Shane made his way around the abandoned store to the street. His car was where he'd left it, untouched by anyone. He checked the glovebox and found his wallet in it as well. Before moving on to anything else, he needed to find a phone and make sure Jacinta was okay.

He returned to the diner he'd stopped at earlier and ambled inside, finding the place nearly completely empty, save for a tired-looking old man in a corner booth.

The waitress behind the counter lifted her head from a tattered paperback she was reading "You look like you need some coffee."

Shane gave her a nod. "Also, where's the bathroom?

"Bathroom's around the back there," she told him, pointing to the far side of the dining area.

Shane grunted his thanks and headed to where she'd indicated. The bathroom was small and cramped, with checkerboard tiles on the floor and the chemical scent of lemon cleanser heavy in the air.

He looked at himself in the mirror and grunted again. Blood from his ear, where Badger had punched him over and over, had dried with dirt. Bloody mud covered most of the right side of his head. The rest of him was just dirty and sweaty. He looked like he'd crawled out of a grave.

Shane washed his face quickly, leaning over the sink and letting the water run and drip off him for a moment while he closed his eyes. He was beginning to really hate Detroit.

When he was finished, he returned to the dining room and a mug of steaming coffee on the counter waited for him next to a little tray of artificial creamers and sugar. He took the coffee as it was and took a sip, and felt the hot liquid burn his lips.

"Do you have a phone?" he asked.

The waitress shook her head. "For customer use? We don't. But here, you can use this one. Just keep it local," she said, pulling a phone out from a shelf behind the counter and setting it in front of Shane. "You alright?"

"Been better," he admitted. "But fine."

She nodded and gave him some privacy as he dialed an operator and got connected to the hospital. It took several minutes before he was redirected to Jacinta's room. The phone rang a couple of times before the line finally clicked.

"Hello?"

"Jacinta," Shane said.

"Shane!" she replied. "Where are you?"

"Diner," he answered. "How are you?"

"I'm fine. My head feels like it's been in a vice, but I'm okay. I tried calling you. What's going on?"

"It's Jessop. He's our guy."

"Chris Jessop?"

"Yeah," Shane confirmed.

"Oh, my God. So it was Jessop who got me in the crash?"

"Yup. And he blames me, blames criminals, blames everyone at the W Four C. Thinks he's a vigilante now."

"He came after you?"

"Tried to. Got close. Closer than I would have liked, anyway. But he's been controlling Price and that Dayton guy."

"He made me call you. And drive into a goddamn tree," she fumed. "I couldn't do anything; it was like being gagged and cuffed."

"Yeah. He seems good at possession. Must have learned some tricks from being held by Hawthorn. I don't know."

"He's lucky he's already dead," she said, and Shane smirked.

"Aggressive. I like it. I'll break one of his fingers on your behalf, I promise," he added. At that, the waitress glanced up from her book.

"Just a finger? Seems a little weak. But what's the plan? How are you going to get him out in the open?"

"Working on it," he answered. "He thinks I'm dead right now. Or trapped in a basement, dying. I have some time to work out a plan."

"In the meantime?"

"Maybe narrow his options down. He'd left Price at her house. I'll drive there to see if she's still locked up."

"He's been doing this to her since when?"

"Since Dayton got fired, I think. Looks like he locks her up when he uses Dayton. When he needs Price, Dayton takes her place in the basement prison I found in her house. Just a whole system Jessop came up with. But if I can get Price out of the way, he'll be stuck with Dayton, and that'll make it harder to get his work done in the halfway house."

"Just watch your back this time, 'kay? Left to die in a basement sounds like he got more than close," she pointed out.

"Like I said, he got close. Didn't work. I'm having coffee now."

"Right. The doctors want me here until the morning, so a few hours at least. Call my cell if anything happens."

"I will," he assured her before hanging up.

"Rough night, huh?" the waitress asked, taking the phone back.

"Something like that." He managed to put on a small smile and thanked her for the phone.

He finished his coffee quickly, and left money on the counter while the waitress was giving the old man in the booth a refill, then headed out.

I need to get to Price before Jessop comes back for her. Her workday would start shortly after sunrise.

Shane had things to do.

CHAPTER 21
ROADBLOCKS

By the time Shane had reached the more secluded and cozy neighborhoods of Detroit, to the house where he'd followed Jessop the day before, the sky was already beginning to lighten. Quiet and unassuming, Jocelyn Price's house fit the persona of an elderly woman who probably had genuinely devoted her life to helping others and being a decent human being. Until Chris Jessop had moved in and used her as a tool to kill.

Shane parked on the street outside the house. Whether or not she was home, he didn't want to draw attention to himself in a way that her neighbors might remember, just in case.

The driveway sat empty. No car only meant Jessop was not in the premises. The only question was whose body he was currently using. Perhaps, it didn't matter, as long as Jessop was not there. Shane didn't want to waste any more time, however.

Shane got out of his car and walked casually across the street. He then followed the same path he'd had the evening before, heading around to the rear of the house and entering through the back door. Nothing in the home looked different from what he recalled. The kitchen remained untouched, as far as he could tell.

Shane headed down the stairs to the basement and approached the door where he'd left Price. He turned the knob and opened it.

The woman on the bed was awake, her eyes wide with terror as Shane entered the room. No doubt she had expected to see Dayton come in. Jessop's ritual had likely been going on for months, with the ghost swapping one body for the other.

"Who are you?" Price demanded, unable to keep the panic out of her voice. "You look... vaguely familiar. But I can't... I don't... Please don't hurt me."

Shane glanced around the room until his eyes fell on a key hanging from a small hook near the door. Out of range of whomever might have been locked up, but easily accessible to Jessop when he needed to switch bodies.

"My name is Shane Ryan. Thought I might help get you out of here," he said. All at once, the look on Price's face switched from fear to a mixture of relief and desperation. She crawled closer to him, holding her wrists out. Her breathing came in great, trembling gasps, and she seemed like she might burst into tears at any moment.

"The key by the door! Please, help me. He'll be back around sunrise. He always comes back!"

Shane took the key from the wall and approached her quickly.

"You have no idea what it's like! He's a... I don't understand. Please, we have to leave. We have to get out of here!"

"What do you know about what's going on?"

She shook her head, violent and dramatic, encouraging him with her hands to get the lock and chains off. "I don't... I don't understand any of it. It's like a force, like a voice that enters my head, and then I wake up in here. And Dayton! Thomas Dayton is part of it! Sometimes he's chained up as well, and I don't—"

"You're being possessed by a ghost. A man named Chris Jessop. But it's okay, we'll get you out of here."

Shane put one hand on the chain to hold it steady, undid the padlock, and loosened the chains. Price stared at him with a nearly unreadable look on her face. The range of emotions had to be overwhelming, and he understood that. Given her line of work, she was probably the kind of person who put a lot of stock in science, in empirical evidence and real word results and facts. This was not only out of her wheelhouse, it was out of her reality.

"You're not the police," she said.

It was a strange thing to point out, but he shrugged. "No, I'm not."

"I don't understand. How... Ghosts aren't real. It's something else. It's..."

"A ghost, Mrs. Price. And he'd been using you to kill residents at the halfway house. Keeping you here to rest your body while he uses Dayton's, then swapping back again."

"No," she said, shaking her head. "No, that's not possible. There's no such thing."

"Suit yourself," Shane told her. "We should still leave, though, shouldn't we?"

"I don't..." she stared at him, her face a mask of confusion and fear. "He's been making me do things for him. Use my position to research people and places and..."

She shook her head, looking down and rubbing her wrists. Her face was flushed red, and her breathing was still irregular. She was going to hyperventilate soon if she didn't calm down.

"It's hard to remember. It's all piecemeal, all jumbled together. Please tell me he didn't make me do anything... bad. I didn't hurt anyone, did I?"

She reached out and grabbed Shane by the hands, her flesh cool and papery against his own. He had seen people coming out of a possession before, and understood the terrible sense of confusion that overcame them, the missing chunks of memory and the feeling that they had been used as puppets. It was not an easy thing to accept, he was sure.

"People were hurt. By him, not by you," he told her. "But we need to leave this place now to prevent him from taking control of you again. Can you do that?"

"Oh my God," she said, covering her own mouth. "The residents. I remember the residents who'd died. He did all that?"

Shane nodded, taking her gently under the arm and helping her get to her feet.

"He did. But I'm planning on stopping him from doing it again. If there's anything you can remember that can help me, that'd go a long way to ending this quickly."

"I don't understand. Who are you? Have we met before?"

"A concerned citizen," Shane replied.

Price shook her head and stammered for a moment, struggling to get hold of any relevant memory as Shane helped her take a step away from the bed. She took a second step and stopped, clutching at his elbow.

"The chemicals," she said, eyes widening. "It was just after this all started, I think. I... bought chemicals."

"What chemicals?" Shane asked.

She shook her head. "I don't know. Solvents. Cleaning supplies? But there were jugs and buckets of them. I... He bought them and had them delivered to the facility. They're hidden in the utility room along with the cleaners and other products there. I don't know what they're for, but there was so much, too much."

Shane wasn't sure what interest Jessop had in chemicals, especially in bulk. It didn't really fit with his MO. But in life, he had been a crime scene cleaner, so he had some understanding of cleaning up bodies. Maybe it was something meant to cover up what he'd done or was about to do. Maybe not. But the quantity was substantial and potentially dangerous.

"Do you know where he might be right now? Is there any place he frequents besides the W Four C?"

Price shook her head once more and began to walk with Shane again.

"He drives around sometimes. In the neighborhood, I think, around the facility. I would wake up in different places, just for a moment, like coming out of a dream. But mostly it was just the facility. He always makes sure we're there on time to start work. He wanted to be there so much, to learn about the residents and talk to them."

Shane nodded and helped her up the stairs. The gaps in her memory were likely too significant for her to offer anything else useful. She just needed to leave the area. For her own safety, sure, but also to limit what Jessop could do. It was on par with disarming an opponent. It would set Jessop back, and hopefully give Shane something more to capitalize on.

Dayton was probably not permitted at the halfway house given his record. If Jessop wanted to get inside, he would need Price. Shane was going to make it difficult for him to do that. His plan could backfire just as easily as it could succeed, and it could prompt him to cut and run, but Shane didn't think it was going to happen. It was a gamble, but he didn't think Jessop was willing to give up.

Shane led the woman out of the stuffy house into the early morning air. The sun had still not yet risen, but it seemed likely Jessop would return soon as Price had mentioned he always did.

"Do you have somewhere you can go to that's safe? Some place he wouldn't know to look?"

"I have Alice," she said, thinking. "My friend Alice lives close by. I haven't talked to her in some time."

"That'll do," Shane said. "You need to keep a low profile for at least a day. Don't contact anyone from work, don't return to your house. And it's best if no one else goes looking for Dayton until I have a chance to get to him. So don't contact the police. He's dangerous. The ghost controlling him is dangerous."

"But who are you?" she asked again. "How can you do anything? How do you even know what's happening?"

"It doesn't matter how I know what I know. Right now, we have to stop him."

Shane took her to his car and drove to her friend's house while she gave directions. Shortly after, they pulled into the driveway of a two-story home with an SUV and a compact car in the driveway. A second-floor light indicated someone was already awake at the early hour.

"Thank you for doing this. For helping me," she told him as they came to a stop.

"Yeah, it's not a problem. You needed to get away from him."

"What do I tell people?" she asked. "What you've told me is too fantastic. Unbelievable. They'll think I've lost my mind if I tell them the truth. I'll be mocked. I'll lose everything. How do I deal with this?"

"You can tell the truth," Shane suggested. "Deal with what comes, but it sounds like you have that pegged already. And honestly, it's even worse than you think. But it is what it is. So you can try it. Or you can lie."

"Still, what lie can explain this?"

Shane could think of at least a dozen off the top of his head, but he'd been dealing with this sort of thing a lot longer than Price and had more practice.

"No doubt neighbors have seen Dayton coming in and out of your house for months now. But you kept coming in and out as well, so no one got too suspicious. Just say Dayton and another man you didn't know were keeping you captive. Say they drugged you, or threatened you, or coerced you, and you were too scared to come forward. Or say nothing. So far, you've done nothing that makes you criminally liable. No one will come for you; the police won't be looking to take you to task for Jessop's crimes."

"Jessop—what is the man's name again? Chris? I don't think I've even met him. Who is he? Why did he do this to me?"

"Truthfully? Convenience. You have access to the facility and nobody would question you digging up information on the residents., That's all."

"Convenience." The woman looked out the window then, still processing what was happening.

"He used you. They do that sometimes. To him you were a tool, that's all. So, like I said, it might be easier to account for it by not accounting for it. Move on as well as you can. Play dumb and say nothing."

"Nothing?" she asked quietly, disgust clear in her voice. "Just pretend it never happened?"

"Yes," Shane answered. "It's a tough pill to swallow, I get that. But you know the alternatives. Like you said, nobody will believe you. Or worse, people will question every decision you've made going back years. But you lived. You're free now. And that's more than a lot of people get. That's more than Jessop got."

"What do you mean?" she asked.

"He was just like you, only worse. The ghost of a serial killer had used him to continue committing murder. And he died in the process. When he returned as a ghost, he took it upon himself to rid the world of criminals. Lumped them all up as no different from the man who'd possessed him."

"My God," Price whispered. "So what happens now, then? There's no police for this. But there's you. What can you do?"

"I can stop him," he answered simply. He didn't need to say more. And as she looked at him, her eyes meeting his, it seemed there was some degree of understanding there. As much understanding as someone like her could have about a world she'd just discovered was real.

"Yes. Please. He needs to be stopped."

Shane nodded but said nothing else.

"Thank you again, Mr. Ryan," she said. "I think I'm just going to… I think I need a drink." She got out of the car and headed for the door of her friend's home. Shane waited until the door opened before pulling out of the driveway. Dayton would be showing up to her house soon, if he hadn't already, Shane was sure.

The noose was tightening for Jessop. If he was smart, he would drop everything and run. It was the best play for self-preservation. But Shane knew that wasn't Jessop's nature. He wasn't smart, and he wasn't going to see the forest for the trees.

Jessop was convinced he was right. He was doing good work, in his own mind. And losing Price would likely just fuel his fire.

Shane hit the road again, heading back toward the halfway house. With Price gone, he would have Jessop on the ropes. And hopefully fully dealt with before the day ended.

Like Price said, he needed to be stopped.

CHAPTER 22

LOCKDOWN

The sun was already cresting the tops of the buildings of downtown Detroit when Shane reached the halfway house. Morning commuters made traffic slow to a crawl, but gave Shane time to ponder scenarios and how he might approach Jessop. The ghost might remain inside of Dayton—or more likely, abandon him and enter the house unseen.

There was a possibility the ghost had scouted another host—maybe a resident that allowed him to remain inside at all hours, when it would be unusual for even Price to be there. There was no lack of suitable candidates available. Many of the residents had traumatic pasts full of violence, drug abuse, and more. Prime real estate for a ghost to stake a claim.

With his plans disrupted, Shane was hoping that Jessop would reveal himself quickly. Maybe attack Shane directly to get revenge. It would make everything easier.

Shane could return as a resident and offer some excuse for where he'd been overnight, something to get him in the door. It didn't matter what, and it wasn't as though breaking curfew had real consequences for him.

In the distance, flashes of light drew his attention several blocks ahead on the road. The police had assembled outside the halfway house. Cars were being redirected as uniformed officers tried to set up blockades.

Shane cursed under his breath and took a right, heading down a sidestreet, along with several other cars that were trying to avoid the traffic jam.

Something had clearly gone wrong. It was possible Jessop could have returned to Price's home already, found her missing, and then panicked in some way.

He took a left and circled around the halfway house, finding more police on the street behind it. The building was effectively surrounded, and the odds of anyone getting in or out were all but gone. Shane needed to find out what was going on and find a way in.

Shane continued past the halfway house, pulling off onto another quiet sidestreet a couple of blocks away. He parked under a tree and sat in the shade, watching the road behind him in the rearview mirror. Traffic was light; most of the redirected cars opted to head around the park rather than behind the house.

After several minutes, he got out and walked back the way he had come. The closest side of the halfway house bordered an alley where deliveries of food and supplies were brought to loading doors off the kitchen. It was wide enough for a truck to enter. The area was mostly obscured by the shadow of the building next door.

A small brick wall separated the alley from a nearly identical alley next to the neighboring building. While a police cruiser had already blocked the kitchen entrance to the halfway house, the neighboring alley sat empty of all but one person.

Shane approached quickly, ducking behind the wall way before any of the police around the W4C saw him. Midway up the alley, the figure sat on the ground, leaning against the wall.

Shane approached the figure casually. It was a man, or had been once. Now he was a ghost, bundled tight with layers of flannel and cotton, and a big army surplus overcoat and a scarf. His beard was scruffy, and he wore a red-and-black checkered cap on his head.

"Hey, you got a second?" Shane asked, coming to the ghost's side. The dumbfounded ghost stared back, his rheumy eyes blinking in confusion.

"You're talking to me," the ghost said. He looked like he might have been in his sixties when he died. His voice was shaky and uncertain. Shane suspected he hadn't spoken in some time.

"Yeah. You know what's happening here?" he asked, nodding toward the halfway house. The ghost reached out a hand slowly, tentatively, and almost touched Shane. Shane watched him warily, not sure what the ghost's plan was, He didn't really have time to deal with another problem.

"You're still alive," the ghost said. Shane nodded. The spirit pulled his hand back, as though realizing the impropriety of his gesture. "It's been... I haven't talked to anyone alive since... I was alive. How about that?"

"I imagine death gets lonely. But this place behind you, any idea what's going on?" Shane asked again.

The ghost craned his neck and looked at the wall. "The wall?" he asked.

"The building on the other side of the wall." Shane's hope for some answers was shrinking by the moment.

"Oh, that. Just a junkie," the ghost answered, shaking his head. "Junkie came back. Used to run the place, but they ran him off. Now he's back. Real piece of work he was. I sometimes sit in during their therapy sessions. Made me feel better, listening to living folks with worse problems than me. That guy's a scumbag. You know, lording over the residents, even telling them to push merch or be taken out of the program—"

"Dayton?" he asked.

The ghost looked at him. "Ohio? You from there? You're accent doesn't—"

"No—that's the name of the former administrator. He was selling drugs here once."

"Sure. Damon." The ghost nodded.

"Did you see what happened?"

"So, again, the junkie came back. Caused a ruckus, from what I heard. Someone called the fuzz. Now the junkie's got hostages. You know how long it's been since someone alive had talked to me?"

"Can't say I do, but you said it's been a while," Shane said, looking up at the halfway house. He could hear blips and static fuzz from the police radio in the alley on the other side of the wall, but nothing came through clearly. He hadn't expected a hostage situation.

"I don't remember exactly," the ghost said. "But it's been a long time. Since I was alive."

"Life is lonely and death is lonelier," Shane told him.

The ghost shook his head. "Nah. Life is lonelier," he corrected. "At least when you're dead, people have an excuse for ignoring you."

Shane looked at him and grunted. "Good point."

"You're not a cop," the ghost observed. "You got something going on here?"

"That junkie's possessed. I'm here to deal with the ghost."

"You mean the guy been making people take the big adios?"

"You've seen him, then."

The grubby spirit nodded.

"In and out a lot. Tried to talk to me a few times. Living people never talk to me. Ghosts? They talk sometimes. They usually haven't got anything good to say. Creeps, for the most part, but nothing crazy. This one, though, I didn't like his vibe. At all."

Shane grunted again before asking, "What's your name?"

The spirit's eyes narrowed, and he looked Shane up and down. "Why do you want to know?"

"So I can call you something. I can call you 'ghost', if you'd rather. Or 'hey you'."

"Edgar," the ghost said. "My name is Edgar. I think. I remember that name. Haven't had to tell anyone in a long time."

"Alright, Ed. I need to get in that place without anyone seeing me. You got any ideas?"

"Edgar," the ghost corrected. "And what do I call you? Chrome Dome?"

"Shane."

"Why do you wanna get into a place like that?" Edgar asked. "Ghost taking hostages. Ghost making people off themselves. Junkies. It's a bad scene."

"Like what I said, I need to deal with the bad vibe ghost. Need to get inside to have a little chat with him."

"Huh." Edgar looked Shane over once again. "'Little chat' usually means something else to people who—look like you."

Shane winced but admitted, "More often than not."

"You can beat up a ghost? I never saw anything like that before."

"If I need to, yeah."

Edgar chuckled at that. "Known a few cocky fellas who could use a head knock or two over the years." Then, after another chuckle, he began to awkwardly get to his feet. He moved a lot like an old man with a sore back, taking time to right himself and look around.

"Normally, you could just slip in a side door like in the kitchen," Edgar continued. "But they locked this place down. I watched 'em test the system when they built it. 'Lockdown protocol', they called it. All doors and windows seal up tight like a prison. It can only be controlled from the inside."

"But they've insisted it's not a prison," Shane said.

Edgar shrugged. "Anyway, none of the doors will open now. Got bars on the windows and these big mechanical locks like a bank vault. Fuzz can't even get in till someone from the inside flips the switch."

"Well, I could really use some help getting in," Shane said. "Jessop will—"

"Jazz what?"

"That's the ghost's name. Jessop." Shane sighed. "He will kill everyone inside."

"You think?" Edgar asked, a frown of concern on his face.

"This is a curveball. Not sure if he's desperate, panicked, or just angry that his plan got derailed. Now he's unpredictable, and I don't want to put anything past him."

"So, you really need someone to flip that switch and get you in."

"But if the person controlling the switch doesn't want anyone in, then it stays locked."

"That's a possibility," Edgar admitted. "What you need is a secret entrance. Some covert spy stuff. You ever watch James Bond?"

"Did someone seriously build a secret entrance to a halfway house?" Shane asked, not convinced such a thing existed.

Edgar chuckled again. "Not so much built one as didn't bother to close one. This place used to be a slaughterhouse, did you know that?"

"I thought that was a block from here? The building they tore down recently?"

"Nah, that was Wincott Meats. This used to be an industrial area a lifetime ago. And these buildings here," the ghost pointed to the W4C and the next-door building, "were a slaughterhouse. Have you ever smelled a slaughterhouse in the height of summer?"

"Can't say as I have, Edgar," he replied.

The ghost nodded. "It stinks, and that's why they had sluice gates and big floor drains and stuff underground. Lots of space down there. Access tunnels in the sewers and what not. Nothing that this place needed, but nothing construction crews would bother to close up, either."

"And how do I get to these tunnels?" Shane asked.

The ghost walked toward the other building, passing through the wall and leaving Shane alone in the alley. A moment later, Edgar emerged again and pointed to Shane's left.

"Door," he said.

Shane grunted and approached a blank beige door. Something clicked on the inside, a lock moving back, and Shane pulled on the knob to find Edgar waiting on the other side.

"There's access in the basement here. This whole block is on the same sewer system underground. I walk around down there sometimes. Not much else to do, you know? There should be a way in from there."

"*Should be?*" Shane asked.

The ghost shrugged. "I'm not a sewer monster; I just walk around there sometimes… Fine. I'll look ahead and see what I can find."

Shane entered the building and paused, listening for any signs of life. He'd passed the place a few times but had paid little attention to it. It was a business that made custom-fitted doors, if he remembered correctly. With police blocking the area, if anyone was coming to open up for the day, they'd likely been held back.

Edgar led him to a cellar door and down a basement full of pipes and the inner works of the plant, including some duct work and various control panels. It looked like a normal industrial basement.

There was storage at the far end of the room. Just outside a caged area holding machine parts that Shane didn't recognize was a large floor grate for drainage.

Edgar pointed at it. "There you go. I'll see you down there."

Then the ghost was gone.

Shane crouched down, slid his fingers into the holes of the grate, and pulled up. It was heavier than it looked. Several minutes of jerking and maneuvering later, he dropped into a cramped tunnel below.

Shane hunched over in the damp and dark tunnel. His eyes adjusted slowly, and he headed in the direction of the halfway house, looking for signs of an entrance—or Edgar.

The cramped tunnel gave way to a junction of larger tunnels, giving Shane the opportunity to stand. Water ran at a slow trickle down the main tunnel, and the place smelled of mildew and stagnant pools. The slightest sound echoed, but at that moment, the only real noises were the running water and Shane's own footsteps.

Edgar then emerged from a branching tunnel to Shane's left. He waved him over.

"Got what you need," he said before disappearing again just as quickly.

Shane made his way to another of the cramped tunnels, hunching down as he walked the length to a section that was dry but smelled old and rotten.

The new length of tunnel was too dark to make out very clearly, but the stench of old death was unmistakable, as was the squeaking and scurrying of rats.

"See it?" Edgar said suddenly in the dark.

"No, Edgar, I don't. We don't have the best lighting here," Shane pointed out.

The ghost scoffed. "You don't have one of them phones with a flashlight? Everyone's got one of those. They're a bit after my time, but I see enough of the living wandering with your heads in 'em—"

"Hold on," Shane cut the ghost off. Jessop had taken his phone when he was captured, but he'd left his lighter.

Shane ignited it and held it up. The space was less like a sewer tunnel and more like a small room. Edgar stood in front of him and pointed up the wall. A steel ladder was affixed to the stone and blocked off by a grate overhead.

"That's your meat drainage floor. They didn't redo the basement," Edgar explained.

"So that's the basement of the halfway house right there?" Shane asked, looking up.

Edgar nodded.

Shane pocketed his lighter before reaching for the ladder. He took a tentative step up, unsure if the rungs were any good after how many years they must have been down there.

Leverage was an issue, but if the ladder rungs held fast, he was in a good position to make the most of his leg muscles. After a deep breath, Shane took another step up, and another, until his back was pressed against the grate in the ceiling. Taking most of the weight on his shoulders, he started to lift up.

The grate dug into his shoulder, but he pushed harder. Something above him creaked, and he felt the grate give very slightly. He doubled his efforts, and the metal clanged.

Shane cursed and hoped no one inside the building had heard. He lifted the entire grate out of his way and crawled into a dark basement.

He was in. He just needed to find Jessop.

And end his madness once and for all.

CHAPTER 23
WHAT GOES AROUND

The walls were lined with shelves of canned tomatoes and beans. There were jugs of vinegar, containers of salt, and boxes of nitrile gloves and sponges.

"Everything okay?" Edgar asked from the darkness below.

"So far, so good," Shane replied.

Shane opened the door and found himself in a larger part of the basement with the backup generator, the heating system and the rest of the machinery needed to keep the house running. He made his way to the stairs and headed up carefully, keeping his footfalls silent.

No sound greeted him as he waited at the top of the stairs. After taking a moment to be sure no one was around, he turned the knob. The smell of chemicals immediately met his nose. It wasn't something he recognized, but it was a strong odor that was clearly hazardous when inhaled.

The hallway beyond was empty, and Shane was not entirely sure what part of the building he was in. He assumed it must be on the kitchen side of the building, but he needed to explore more to get oriented.

He made his way cautiously down the hall. He could hear muffled shouts and thuds from elsewhere in the facility, distant and impossible to make out. At the early hour, most would have still been in their rooms, with just a few out and about, like those on kitchen duty or with early morning jobs to get to.

If Jessop had taken hostages, then they'd likely be in a place where he could keep an eye on everyone, and with no access from outside.

Most likely the cafeteria. It had outside windows, and had only two entrances, both on the same wall. It would be a good place to round up the hostages.

The chemical smell grew stronger as Shane continued walking to a windowless door. It clicked quietly and fell open when he turned the handle. He found himself in the kitchen.

The cafeteria was visible from the kitchen through a large window along the chow line, where residents lined up to have their trays filled with the daily culinary atrocity. Shane kept low to avoid detection and made his way toward it, standing only once he'd reached the cover of the wall dividing the two rooms.

He sneaked behind a stack of trays between the chow line window and a set of swinging doors to get a full view of the cafeteria. Dayton stood with his back to Shane, a gun in his hand. Kitchen monitors and a handful of residents, all in kitchen whites and hairnets, sat at the tables. Abbott was also there. In the corners were containers with labels Shane couldn't read from the distance.

The chemical smell was getting too overwhelming now. Shane was already feeling slightly lightheaded. Then he noticed small puddles of clear liquid all over the floor, as though it had been splashed about on purpose.

Crouching, Shane touched the nearest wet patch and then brought his fingertips to his nose. He squinted and then wiped his hands on his pants, the smell stinging his nostrils. Definitely a solvent of some kind—maybe a mix of compounds. Whatever it was, it was flammable.

Shane pushed open the doors and walked out slowly. He didn't have a lot of options when it came to attacking Jessop. If nothing else, he might buy some time to come up with a better plan.

Dayton heard the doors swinging and turned just as Shane had entered the room. His eyes widened, but only just, the gun moving from the assembled crowd of hostages to Shane.

"Took you longer than I expected."

Shane couldn't tell if he was trying to play it cool, or if he'd legitimately expected Shane to show up. Either way, it didn't matter. Shane raised his hands and took a few steps toward Dayton.

"Had to kill a badger in the basement, then I drove a sweet old lady to a friend's house." Shane winked.

Dayton's lips pursed very slightly.

"God. You're the most exceptional man in the world, aren't you?"

"I don't know about that," Shane said. "I'm just a regular guy. You— you're on a crusade to end all evil after your guts exploded. Now that's special."

"How about you take a seat before your brains explode out the back of your head?"

Shane wrinkled his nose. "No thanks. I'd rather stand."

"Sit or you die," Dayton warned.

Shane sighed. "You're going to shoot me now, just before the climax of your biggest performance yet, just because I won't sit? I don't know if I buy that. It seems like you've been waiting for me. You want me to watch the entire thing unfold."

Dayton turned the gun away, his eyes still locked on Shane, and shot one of the hostages. The bullet tore through the man's chest. He collapsed, and Abbott rushed to his aid.

Dayton pulled the hammer back on the gun.

"Leave him," he shouted.

The monitor turned to face him. "He's going to die."

"That's the point." Dayton aimed the gun at the monitor. "Now sit, or you're next."

Abbott did as he was told. Dayton kept the gun trained at him but spoke to Shane. "Now, do you want to keep standing or should I clear another seat for you?"

The chairs were closer to Dayton than where Shane had chosen to stand. He narrowed the distance by several feet as he walked to a chair, pulling it from a table and turning it just enough so that he was directly facing the hostage-taker.

"Good man," Dayton said.

Shane smiled as his hand drifted into his jacket. The gun was on him in an instant.

"Stop right there!" Dayton shouted.

Shane moved slowly, retrieving the pack of cigarettes from his pocket. "You mind? I figured, if you're going to kill me anyway, I might as well have a smoke first."

"You're not going to want to light that in here," Jessop assured him. Shane paused, a stick halfway to his lips. The solvent smell was as strong in the cafeteria as it was in the kitchen.

Dayton nodded toward the buckets in the corner. "You can learn a lot from doing crime scene clean up, you know? Not just about what solvent you might need to clean human blood out of a carpet, or cement, or untreated wood. But also what kinds of things people use to hide their crimes. Chemicals that can burn off a person's fingerprints, or even dissolve a whole body. Compounds that can melt through metal, or burn a whole building in just minutes."

"Right," Shane said, putting the cigarette back in its pack. "So, you're going to torch us all, huh?"

"Why not? You all deserve it. This jerk Dayton deserve it."

Shane glanced at the others in the room. "Thought you hated criminals? The scum of the earth, blah blah blah. What's your beef with these monitors?"

Dayton's lips twitched but he did not say anything.

"I know I'd rather not be burned alive. You can jump into a furnace for all I care, though."

"I think it's appropriate," Dayton gushed. "This is how it all started after all."

"Maybe dramatic is the word you're looking for."

"Fire!" Dayton continued, like he hadn't heard Shane's dig. "The gas station fire where Hawthorn had died—I guess, in a way—was also where I died. It was the last place I was truly me, wasn't it? Before he took over, made me come here, made me do those atrocities. And then you killed me, so I never had a chance to be me again. You killed us both there. And now I'll bring it full circle."

Shane held up a finger. "First off, I didn't kill Hawthorn. One of his victims did. Second, he didn't die in the fire. He was dead before the fire torched his body. But whatever makes your fantasy more exciting would also work, I guess."

"You talk too much. One more reason to kill you."

"Then what? You go out and play Batman some more? Fighting crime under the cover of an old lady?"

"Don't worry about it, Shane. You'll be dead anyway."

"Yeah, I get that part of your plan. I guess where you're losing me is the end. What's your ultimate goal? You're just going to kill every criminal within a ten-block radius of a rundown part of Detroit? So what? Who cares?"

"People will care! The people whose lives I've saved will care. I can see why that means nothing to you."

"Oh, right. The people that Clem drove by too fast as a getaway driver from a robbery never have to worry about being splashed by felonious puddles again."

Shane laughed, and Dayton aimed the gun directly at his head.

"You must really want to die," he said quietly.

Shane shrugged. "Try me."

No one else in the room spoke, but Shane had no doubt they were as confused by the conversation as they were afraid of what Jessop, or "Dayton", had planned to do next. When it was all said and done, they could chalk it up to Dayton being high or mentally disturbed. Assuming there were survivors.

"I wonder, what was your plan today, Shane?"

"Me? Just wanted to talk. See where your head is at," Shane replied.

Dayton nodded. "I feel like you thought you'd come in here with your little attitude, and somehow kill me and save the day. Ride off into the sunset with the girl, that sort of thing. Is that about right?"

"Sounds like you spend a lot of time thinking about me."

"Yeah, that's the attitude I'm talking about. Such a tough guy. All scarred up and ugly. Smoking cigarettes. I bet you were in the army or something."

"Or something."

Shane knew he needed to close the gap. Getting Jessop all worked up seemed like the best course. Maybe he'd get closer on his own, come in to try to take a swipe at Shane. Or maybe get sloppy for a moment. Maybe let his guard down long enough for Shane to rush at him. If he could catch him off guard, it'd only take a couple of steps.

"Yeah, well, see if any of that helps you with this."

Jessop raised his other hand, his thumb moving as he did so. Shane had only a moment to notice before the flame in Jessop's hand flicked to life and the lighter sailed away from his fingers.

The hostages screamed, panic and anger taking over as they fell back or tried to get away from their chairs. Instinctively, Shane pushed off with his heels. The chair skidded back across the floor as Dayton blindly fired his gun at everyone.

In seconds, the lighter hit the floor and fire roared to life. It raced along the trails of chemicals, engulfing the tables in the center of the room, racing across the floor to the kitchen and climbing the walls all around them. It spread faster than any fire Shane had ever seen.

And total chaos followed.

Chapter 24
The Conflagration

As the pools of chemicals ignited, flames raced up the walls in the cafeteria and adjacent kitchen. Jessop fired off every round of his gun, hitting some of hostages as they fled. When the gun clicked empty, the man locked eyes with Shane across a wall of fire and smiled.

Dayton's body collapsed as Jessop separated himself from his living host. The far door to the cafeteria was already blocked by fire that had spread to the floor and the ceiling. The doorway nearest Shane was still passable.

"That way," Shane shouted over the sound of screaming men and crackling fire. He directed the others to the door before heading in the opposite direction to check on Dayton.

The fire was moving too fast and unpredictably. It followed the irregular pattern of the liquid that had been splashed about. Swirls of hot air, searing, blinding and painful, buffeted Shane from all angles as they moved and flowed in currents.

Aside from the heat, the smell from the solvent as it burned brought tears to his eyes. The smoke felt thick and irritating in his throat. Shane tried to ignore it as he made his way to Dayton's limp body.

The man was still alive, but unconscious. Shane tried to wake him with no luck, first shouting his name, then resorting to slapping his face. It did nothing, and the man remained unconscious, breathing but immobile, as the flames spread closer.

"Grab this guy," Shane shouted to the nearest of the monitors, a man crawling away from a burning table towards the exit.

The man looked at Shane like he was crazy.

"Screw him," the monitor said before turning and running for the open door, shielding his face from the flames as others in the room followed suit.

Shane cursed then lifted Dayton's body and balanced him over a shoulder before making his way for the door. Fire licked at both of them. He could smell the man's hair burning as he carried him across a patch of burning liquid before making it to the doors.

The hallway outside provided little relief from the smoke, but the fire had yet to spread fully, mostly sticking to the doorframes leading out of the cafeteria.

The space was full of the men from the cafeteria as well as those who had been in their individual rooms; some banging on the barred windows, others trying to slam their way through exit doors that had been sealed as part of the facility's lockdown protocol.

"This way!" Shane shouted, as he headed toward where he'd first entered the building. He flagged down a couple of kitchen workers and Abbott, getting them to finally come closer to him. The fire had already gotten bigger outside the cafeteria by the time he reached the end of the hallway, licking the walls and floors, a growing inferno.

"Ryan, what the hell is going on?" Abbott demanded. "Why are you saving Dayton? What was that conversation all about? It doesn't make sense!"

"Do you really care about those things right now? Take them to the basement, in the room being used as food storage. There's an open grate there leading to the sewer tunnels. It's the only way out."

"What?" Abbott said, shaking his head.

Shane dumped Dayton on the floor in front of him. "Take him with you. Just trust me. Leave. Now. Round up whoever you can before this whole place goes up."

He pushed past Abbott, but only a step before the monitor grabbed his sleeve. "Where the hell are you going?"

"Got a mess to clean up. Leave while you can, Abbott."

Shane pulled away and ran down the hall, grabbing men as he went and pushing them back the way he'd come with instructions to follow Jack Abbott. More residents had come out of their rooms. Whatever else happened, Jessop had succeeded in causing damage and taking lives again. Now Shane had to make sure it was his last hurrah.

Outside, sirens blared. Shane could see police and paramedics through the windows, backing away from the building. Black smoke rolled heavily along the halls, making it hard to breathe. Shane hunched low as he ran, covering his face with his shirt and squinting against the acrid smoke.

Jessop would have no reason to flee the building. All he needed to do was avoid Shane, go somewhere that the living couldn't follow. That could be anywhere in the fire, though. The longer Shane remained inside, the more likely it would be that he'd succumb to the fire or smoke.

As he made his way down the front hall, past the main entrance and then back toward the therapy rooms, the only movements he saw were residents trying to escape. Jessop was still nowhere to be found.

Shane could have left with the others, headed back through the sewers and out onto the street. But then he'd have to wait for the building to be taken entirely by the flames, and then for everyone to leave before he could even hope to sneak back into the rubble. By that point, Jessop would have been able to escape to any number of places.

"You still in here?" a voice asked as Shane approached the stairwell.

Edgar popped out from inside a wall. Shane coughed rather than answering. The ghost shrugged. "Nevermind. The ghost went up to the roof."

Shane looked from the spirit to the stairs. It would be the most stupid place for anyone living to go when the building was burning down.

Even when he was still alive, in the short time they'd interacted, Jessop had really been a coward. All he did back then was whine and wallow in self-pity, which had made the investigation even harder for Shane and Jacinta. As a ghost, he seemed incapable of acting openly or with much clear intent. He hid and sneaked about; he made people hurt themselves rather than taking any direct attack against them. Hiding in the smoke and fire on the roof fit his pattern well.

Shane pushed the door to the stairwell, then closed it behind, cutting off the worst of the smoke. Edgar joined him, looking up the set of stairs that covered four floors and then a final flight to the roof.

"I think he's alone," the ghost said.

Shane nodded, spitting the taste of chemical smoke out of his mouth and wiping his eyes on his sleeve. "Yeah, he should be."

"You, uh, need any help?"

Shane grabbed the railing and glanced at Edgar. "Could use a set of eyes that don't get blinded by smoke."

The ghost nodded and straightened his jacket. "It's been a while since I had to do something useful. Nice way to get the blood pumping, so to speak."

They ascended the stairs together, even as the smoke began to thicken and rise in swirling clouds around them. The sounds of sirens continued outside, a faint wailing in the distance that grew louder the further up the stairs they went.

The smoke had grown thick, obscuring much of the way up. The fire had not yet spread to that side of the building, but he had no doubt it would get there soon. The accelerant had done a good job of setting the building ablaze quickly and efficiently. It gave Jessop the best chance to keep himself hidden away and kill as many people as possible.

But with luck, Abbott would be able to get most of the residents and employees to escape through the sewers. Jessop's plan would mostly be a failure, and Shane wanted to make sure the ghost knew it. Petty, perhaps, but he still felt like Jessop deserved it.

For a time, Shane had felt almost sympathetic to Jessop. But the ghost had chosen a path of hardship. He had a chip on his shoulder and a broken idea in his mind, which he wanted to see through at any cost.

The air on the roof was a mix of searing heat and jarring cold. The sound of the outside world was all chaos, with shouts and screams melding with honking horns and sirens from emergency vehicles. It was like stepping out into a dozen nightmares all at once. It was all he could do to maintain his balance as he tried to orient himself in the churning blackness.

"Look out!" Edgar shouted from behind him. Shane turned, trying to see the spirit through the smoke, but coming up with little more than flashes of color and shape. He thought he saw Edgar there, at the top of the stairs.

But by then, it was already too late.

CHAPTER 25

PAIN

Something hit Shane violently on his left side. He fell hard onto the rooftop. The surface of the roof was gritty and rough, but strangely sticky. It felt like gravel embedded in tar, hot and jagged against his flesh as his cheek scraped over it. He felt the grit cut into him even as the pressure on his side subsided.

"I knew you'd be too full of yourself to leave," Jessop shouted over the cacophony of noise. Shane opened his eyes and saw the spirit leaning over him.

"Just came here to let you know party's over for you," Shane told him.

Jessop's foot came down hard on Shane's gut, and he coughed, doubling over as a spasm of pain rolled across his body.

"You could have died peacefully, Shane. Could have stayed in the basement of Bolo's house. That would have been a dignified death, you know. Beaten and forgotten. There's nothing wrong with being beaten. And I beat you." He kicked Shane again, higher this time, right under the ribcage.

Shane coughed once more. The smoke played havoc with his vision, obscuring Jessop one moment and burning his eyes the next, leaving whatever he could see a painful blur.

Smoke rolled over his face, and with it came Jessop once more. The ghost was down at Shane's side, his face hovering as he grabbed Shane by the head and slammed it against the rooftop. The skeletal grin was as wide as ever, the edges of his twisted mouth glistening red, like freshly carved meat.

Shane gritted his teeth and lashed out with a left, making contact. He couldn't see where he'd hit Jessop, but the blow was enough to make the ghost back off.

"Having trouble seeing?" A flash of heat followed his words, then the sound of something crunching. Then Shane felt the entire roof shaking.

A segment of the roof collapsed, and black smoke rushed outward. The space was cleared for a moment, long enough to show flames burst up into the sky, freed from their confines. With the collapse of the roof, the fire grew wilder as oxygen was sucked into the building.

Shane noticed some areas of the roof, those far from the door, were devoid of smoke. If he could get there, he'd be able to see the ghost coming. He just needed to get away far enough before the entire ceiling collapsed.

Another kick from Jessop sent him rolling over, forcing him to clutch his ribs and stomach as he gritted his teeth.

Another laugh came from the ghost. "If anything, you should be helping me. You're trying to save criminals, for God's sake. You don't make any sense. You have no sense of justice. At least I'm trying to make the world a better place. What's your purpose?"

Shane let out a growl that ended in a fit of coughing as more of the acrid smoke rolled over him. Ignoring the ghost, he kept crawling forward, trying to get to his knees even as another kick took him in the gut, causing him to fall over again.

"You usually have so much to say," Jessop taunted.

The smoke broke in an updraft and gave Shane a view of a clear spot. He scrambled toward it, looking for a moment's reprieve to regain his footing and square off with the ghost. He pushed his way to the break in the smoke, which was near the edge of the roof overlooking the alley where he'd first met Edgar.

Cold hands fell on Shane as he reached his target. Jessop gripped him at the collar and pushed him just enough to keep him hanging by the edge of the roof.

"What do you think, Shane? Dead from a fall after jumping from the burning rooftop, trying to save his own life? That's actually more honorable than you deserve."

Instead of answering, Shane reached back as the ghost shifted his weight forward. He knew there was a chance the push would land him by the brick wall separating the alleys below. At best, it would leave him crippled, but he would most likely be dead.

Shane's hand clasped Jessop's wrist, and he dug his fingers in with every ounce of strength he could muster.

The momentum of the push, of gravity taking Shane's weight as he was released, dragged the ghost along with Shane. He reached out with his other hand and took hold of Jessop's arm, working the appendage like a short, rough pendulum. It swung Shane back against the building with a thud that knocked the breath from him and caused spots to dance before his eyes.

Pain shot through Shane's ribs and gut where Jessop had kicked him earlier. But he held fast, clutching the spirit's wrist to keep him from falling.

Below, people screamed. At first, Shane thought he'd been seen, that people were watching him hang from an invisible limb on the rooftop in a display he'd never be able to adequately explain. But it was not the case.

Amidst the swirling smoke, fire crews had managed to break through the security doors at the front of the building. To shouts from rescue workers and spectators below, residents who had not escaped with Abbott flooded out.

As the doors opened, another gout of fire burst up through the roof of the building somewhere beyond Jessop. Shane couldn't see how much of the roof might have collapsed, but he could see the spire of flame rise into the sky.

"That was good," Jessop said.

The ghost's nearly blank face hovered over Shane's own, looking down at him without eyes, seeing without seeing.

"Wait 'til you see my next trick," Shane replied.

"You're still going to die here, Shane. I can stay here all day. Can you? 'Til the smoke fills your lungs again? 'Til it sears your eyes blind? 'Til the flames crawl down your hands until you can't bear it anymore and you finally let go? You're good as dead now."

"You're very confident for a man with no face."

"I want you to know something, Shane," Jessop hissed. His voice was steady, unaffected by the smoke or the stress of holding on.

"Do tell," Shane grunted. If he could get the ghost to lean in just a little more, he might be able to get a grip on his shoulder to pull himself up.

"When you're broken down there, when you're dead, I'm going to wait for her to show up. When she hears you're dead, I know she'll come for you."

Shane's eyes scanned the ledge. It was within reach. But it would give Jessop a chance to react if he let him go. It would be hard to get up without the ghost fighting back.

"When Jacinta gets here, I'm going to take her again, just like I did before. What do you think is broken in there, Shane? What made it so easy for me to possess her?" Jessop's voice had a tone of cruelty and spite. "I'm going to make her my pet. Do you know what I'm going to do next? Ask me, Shane."

Shane grunted, digging his nails deeper into the ghost flesh.

"Ask me," Jessop repeated.

Shane said nothing, and just stared at the ghost while finding his footing on the wall beneath him. The brick provided friction, but not much of it. Something to kick off of, certainly.

"I'm going to torture her from the inside, Shane. I'm going to find out what a human body can endure, then break her. And it will be your fault. Because you couldn't leave well enough alone. Because you couldn't take the time to care about anyone or anything around you. Your actions got me killed. Now your actions are going to get her killed, too."

They were just words, Shane knew. Empty threats from a cruel and desperate man, a jaded ghost who had been broken by his own death and now lashed out at anything he felt threatened with. It was not unusual. It was not rare. But it would not stand.

Shane's anger was twisted deep inside him. He could feel it there, always, simmering like any other emotion. He controlled it, as he controlled all parts of himself. He had learned discipline long ago. But Jessop was looking to test that, and Shane was willing to let him.

"Everyone escaped, Jessop," Shane finally said. "Just you and me left. So I think it's time you find out what my purpose is."

Jessop was about to speak again when Shane made his move. With feet braced against the wall, he pushed himself up and reached for Jessop's neck. He pulled as hard and as fast as he could, kicking along the way.

The ghost cried out, more in surprise than anything else. Shane slammed an elbow down against the exposed jaw, breaking a few teeth as he scrambled up Jessop's body.

Once he was up and over the ledge, he moved quickly, rolling and taking Jessop with him. He flipped the ghost, then slammed him down onto his back.

They struggled until Jessop got his hands on Shane's neck, locking it in a frozen, powerful grip. He pulled Shane closer.

"I want to watch the life leave your eyes," Jessop growled, his face inches from Shane's own. Shane's lips parted as he grabbed the ghost by the head, bringing him even closer.

Mouth open, Shane bit down on the side of Jessop's face. He bit as hard as he could, chewing off a piece of the ghost.

Jessop shrieked, and his body spasmed. The effort caused the ghostly flesh to tear. He stopped squeezing Shane's throat and instead pushed him off. The hole in Jessop's face was cavernous. Had he been alive, it would have coated him in blood.

Shane spat out the bit of flesh he tore off the ghost even as it disappeared, and got to his feet.

Half of the roof along the back wall was burning and sending smoke up in black, impenetrable sheets. Parts of the center were collapsing. They had very little time, Shane was sure, before the entire roof collapsed.

Jessop got to his feet as well, going towards Shane, touching the spot on his face that Shane had torn free.

"You should have destroyed me when you had the chance," the ghost said.

Shane smiled at him. "What the hell do you think I'm about to do?"

CHAPTER 26
SILENCED

The wail of sirens continued unabated. Great bursts of water railed against the building as firefighters fought to contain the blaze that Jessop had started. From where Shane stood, it was unlikely that anyone on the street would see him through the fire or the smoke.

"Told you everyone escaped." He pointed to the side of the building, to the alley where Edgar had let him into the building. Abbott was at the door, still guiding residents and staff out through the alley.

Jessop's faceless head glanced down at them.

"Is that your purpose?" he asked. "To save criminals from a just end? You're utterly irredeemable."

Shane laughed. "Your stupid quips are the gift that keeps on giving. I almost want to keep you around. But this roof is collapsing soon, so I'm just going to destroy you now."

"You don't care about the consequences of your actions. Letting Dayton go. The man was running drugs out of here. Saving all those criminals from the fire. Every one of them is scum, but you're the worst of all," Jessop shouted.

Shane shrugged. He was done talking.

"The next Hawthorn could be down there. You don't know—"

But Shane was already in motion. He had stopped caring what Jessop had to say some time ago. He closed the gap between them then brought his right hand across what was left of the ghost's face, clipping the ghost's jaw as hard as he could.

Jessop almost fell back from the force of the blow, but Shane held him up with his other hand, raining down a second and a third punch into the center of his face.

Jessop's attempts to fight back were messy and uncoordinated. He'd caught Shane by surprise before, and therefore had an advantage. Now, head-to-head, he was not prepared for the onslaught.

In life, Jessop had not been a fighter. He was not physically intimidating, and he didn't carry himself like a man who had ever had to fight. Being dead had given him courage. And madness that allowed him to be cruel and brutal. He relied on surprise and subterfuge, his victims never saw him coming. But Shane saw him quite clearly now.

There was something in Jessop's weakness, in his cowardice, that seemed to make his cruelty more pronounced. Tiny Man Syndrome, Shane had heard it called before. That bravado of a bully, relying on something to conceal his cowardice. In Jessop's case, it was being dead. No one could hurt him anymore. No one could even see him. Except Shane still could.

He let Jessop collapse and brought his knees down into the ghost's gut, pinning him in place. His fists did not stop. Jessop had used up all his time and he had ran out of patience. Dead or not, twisted by the trauma of dying and coming back, none of it mattered anymore. Shane's well of sympathy was not deep at the best of times. And it was dry now.

He belted Jessop across the face with a backhand, then balled his fist once more, bringing it down over where the ghost's eyes should have been, then his nose, then his mouth once more.

Jessop flailed like an animal trying to get free as he cried out and squealed. His hands slapped and swung wildly. Shane caught one by the fingers, jerking back and down as hard as he could, snapping three of them straight back.

The ghost wailed, and Shane pulled as hard as he could, holding Jessop's throat down with the other hand. He tore the fingers entirely free and released them, letting them tumble and fizzle from existence before they even landed on the roof.

Jessop gnashed his broken teeth and snarled like a beast caught in a trap, desperate and panicked and devoid of anything close to rationality.

Shane struggled to hold his prey still. But it didn't matter how wild Jessop became. Shane's anger was greater now, burning brighter with every passing moment. The ghost had triggered something in him, crossed a line that could not be uncrossed.

The ghost tried to wriggle away like an insect fleeing a predator, flipping onto his stomach and scurrying towards the safety of the approaching fire, where his tormentor could not follow. Shane knew he couldn't let Jessop escape, couldn't let him hide in the fire, collect himself, and plot a new attack.

The journey that started with Hawthorn back in Canada had been a long one, with too many close calls. Shane had nearly died, and so had Jacinta, more than once. He was tired of it. He was frustrated by it. And more than anything, he was enraged.

Shane fell on Jessop's back as the ghost scuttled across the smoky roof. His left arm crossed over Jessop's face. His grip was tight and powerful, and with his weight holding the ghost down, he arched his back and pulled the ghost's head back.

The ghost reached back, blindly trying to scratch Shane's face or arms or anything to fight back.

"You're going to die here, Shane! I beat you! I beat—"

The ghost's words were cut short as Shane's fist slammed into his mouth once again. He then clutched at Jessop's lower jaw. His thumb looped under the chin as he braced his other arm even more tightly around the faceless head. He pulled as hard as he could, yanking open Jessop's jaw until it came away in Shane's hand with a loud crunch.

The sound that rose from Jessop's open throat was inhuman, a wet and ululating thrum. Shane placed his now free hand on the back of the ghost's head and slammed down with all his might. The ghost's skull collapsed. Shane was thrust backward, spiritual energy bursting around him and launching him towards the stairwell door, through a cloud of ever-thickening smoke.

Shane landed hard and lay still for a moment as he struggled to catch his breath. The creaking of wood and plaster rose over the crackle of flames. A massive section of the roof along the rear wall caved, and for an instant, Shane thought the entire thing would give way.

"You probably don't want to stay here," Edgar said. The ghost's face came down out of the smoke, hovering next to Shane.

"You're still here?" Shane asked, coughing.

"Best fight I've seen in years. Wasn't going to leave midway," he replied. "Come on. You can still get out if you're quick."

Shane followed the old ghost and pulled his shirt collar up to cover his nose and mouth. The stairwell was a wall of darkness. It was impossible to see where he was going.

"Just follow my lead. I'll get you to the sewer," the ghost said.

With Edgar tugging his jacket, Shane made his way blindly down the stairs. He stumbled, all but blind, having to nearly crawl down the stairs while Edgar shouted directions or physically pulled him towards doors.

They reached the main floor but the hallway leading to the basement was engulfed in flames, blocking their exit. Shane crouched low to the floor and cursed. Edgar gave him a pat on the shoulder, then pointed to the wall. A large red fire extinguisher was still affixed in place.

"Really?" Shane asked.

The ghost shrugged. "Got a better idea?"

Coughing and squinting against the rolling smoke, Shane reached for the extinguisher and pulled the pin to free the nozzle. He moved quickly, spraying down as much of the fire in his path as he could.

With a path cleared momentarily, Shane ran, Edgar yanking on his jacket to keep him on track. He barreled into scorching darkness while blasting the extinguisher wildly in all directions to keep himself from being consumed.

As quickly as he'd entered the blaze, he was out again. He tossed the extinguisher aside and made his way to the basement. Behind him, the sound of more wood snapping preceded a massive crash. He moved as fast as his feet could carry him until he reached the storage closet and the open grate in the floor.

Now he just had to walk through the underworld, and he'd be safe.

CHAPTER 27
THE BURNOUT

Shane emerged from the building next to the W4C. He was covered in soot, and some sewer filth as well. He looked like a train wreck, he was sure, but no one was paying attention to him or the building.

There was a substantial crowd across from the halfway house, held back by the police as fire crews worked to contain the blaze as best as they could. More of the roof had collapsed, and the place where he had fought Jessop no longer existed.

He could see ambulances near the park entrance as well, doors open as they treated the victims. Abbott was among them, and a few others that Shane recognized.

His eyes scanned the crowd, and he was able to pick out the park ghost, unseen by everyone else, watching the fire burn. And then, moving through the crowd was another familiar face. Denise Sandoval stopped to talk to a uniformed officer about something.

Shane turned and adjusted his jacket. He could walk wide of the building, circle back, and get to his car.

"You leaving?" Edgar asked.

"Not much else I can do here."

"You have a point there. Good work, I have to say. Really eye-catching."

"I do what I can. And I appreciate the help, Edgar."

"Appreciate someone talking to me." The ghost grinned. "Been doing nothing for too many years."

Shane nodded. Losing time as a ghost was a problem—how one day became two then became ten then became a thousand.

"Make the most of what you have," Edgar continued. "You don't want to die and come back, get stuck in an alley for fifty years, regretting what you could have done while still alive."

"Good advice," Shane told him. And he meant it. There was something to be said for actually living. The anger he had felt, that rage that Jessop had inspired in him, had only confirmed it further.

What was the point of what he was doing with his life, really? He needed to do something different. Soon, too.

Reaching into his pocket, Shane pulled a cigarette from the pack. It was slightly crushed after his fight, but it would still be usable. Edgar snickered, but said nothing.

"See you around, Edgar," Shane said.

The ghost nodded, then turned away to watch the fire as Shane walked away.

He made his way to the nearest side street, then up the block, to where he'd parked his car. He'd need to clean himself up a bit somewhere, but he needed to get to the hospital as well. He needed to make sure Jacinta was okay and let her know what happened.

And then maybe he'd do something crazy.

EPILOGUE

Thomas Dayton was unconscious in the hospital bed, a respirator mask affixed to his face. Monitors beeped and the sound of oxygen shushed through pipes that kept him alive. His wrist was cuffed to a bed rail.

Witnesses from the halfway house, both residents and monitors, had pegged Dayton as the ringmaster of what would go down as one of the most brazen cases of arson and attempted mass murder in history.

According to TV reports, Dayton forced his way to the building and placed it on lockdown, before holing up in the cafeteria with several hostages who had been there before he arrived. But at the last minute, Dayton collapsed, possibly from too much exposure to the chemicals he had used as accelerant. A quick-thinking W4C employee named Jack Abbott had led the people to safety through the sewers, even carrying their unconscious hostage-taker on his back to save the man's life. To the victims, as well as the entire city of Detroit, Jack Abbot was a hero.

Shane and Jacinta stood outside the door, a few paces from the uniformed officer assigned to guard the man. He had been admitted with severe smoke inhalation, and some burns and wounds that wouldn't be life-threatening, but would still keep him in the hospital for a few days.

"You still stink like smoke," Jacinta said, but stood close by his side anyway. He'd cleaned up in a hospital bathroom and was looking better now, though his clothes would need a serious run through a washing machine. He'd spent most of the day in the hospital with Jacinta, without much of a chance to do anything else. It could wait.

"Occupational hazard," he joked.

He'd been officially charged with murder, arson, attempted murder, and additional drug charges. Most of the previous deaths were still regarded as suicides, but the deaths associated with his hostage-taking—the man he'd shot, and those who weren't able to escape the blaze—were going to fall on Dayton.

"Prosecutor is going to push for a life sentence on this. Twelve counts of first-degree murder, and one count of attempted murder for everyone who escaped the building. That's close to one hundred charges," Jacinta said.

Shane grunted. It wasn't technically the fairest deal, but Dayton still wasn't a good man. The drug stuff had been all him; using the W4C residents to sell drugs so he could fund his own addiction had happened before Jessop entered the picture. Part of what made him vulnerable to the possession was his own drug use in the first place.

"And it looks like they are going to make an example of him and will go hard on his prosecution."

Shane could tell she was not happy about the situation. He had told her the whole story after he'd arrived and they spent some time together. As a detective guided by her morals, she didn't see the justice in Dayton taking the fall for Jessop's crimes. But she knew as well as Shane that "a ghost did it" was not going to hold up in a court of law. As far as Shane was concerned, he brought it on himself. It was a better outcome than another totally innocent person taking the fall or even dying. All things being equal, he was at peace with it.

"Could have been worse," he pointed out.

"He'll spend the rest of his life in jail," she countered, though not angrily.

"Could have died, too. He almost did. No one wanted to save him."

"True," she cenceded. "So, do you think this is it?"

"It?" he asked.

"Hawthorn started this, and Jessop took up the torch. We're not going to be fighting off one of Jessop's enraged victims in a few months, are we?"

He hoped not. However, he'd thought it was over long ago when Hawthorn was destroyed. When dealing with things that didn't seem to make sense under the rules of the normal world, it was hard to speak in absolutes.

Shane looked at her then, her head still bandaged from the wound in the car crash. The world had been trying to kill both of them pretty consistently lately, it seemed. There was darkness around them at all times, him especially. Things that were always just out of sight, but never willing to leave him at peace. But he still felt like things hadn't been all that bad.

There was a time in Shane's life when he had mostly lost any drive or purpose. And he had to admit that if not for Jacinta Perez, he might have continued down that path. Being surrounded by death had a way of making life sour.

With Hawthorn, and with Jessop, things had gotten too close too many times.

"I've been thinking," he said to her, glancing around the hospital hallway. It smelled like any other hospital, like sickness mixed with strong disinfectant. He wondered if it was the best place for what he had in mind.

"What's wrong?" she asked, concern on her face.

"Just one thing," he answered. His instincts were that this would backfire on him. That he was going to look foolish. "I was thinking that I wake up every day with the chance of dying. Not just now. It's been that way for as long as I can remember."

Jacinta's eyes reflected a mild degree of confusion. She wasn't used to Shane talking like that. Shane wasn't used to talking like that.

"And?" she said quietly.

"Well, I think it'd be better to wake up every day with something to live for. And I guess most guys do this differently, but who gives a damn? We've been through things I don't think anyone else has experienced. So, why not do one more crazy thing?"

He could feel himself stalling, and he didn't like it. The thought was almost funny. Part of him knew this was never the guy he expected to be. Never even wanted to be. But he also knew he wanted her. And he didn't want to die, or lose her, without grabbing hold of what they had.

"Shane, get straight to the point."

"I just want to make sure you understand. It's not... this isn't something I thought I'd be doing."

"I know," she said. She smiled, her fingers reaching for the pendant on the necklace she always wore.

For just an instant, Shane felt the faintest hint of cold, but it was gone as quickly as it had come.

"We're a lot different," she laughed, looking down for a moment. "But not in the ways it counts. In the ways that do, we are a lot alike. And that's what matters, right?"

He had to agree with that. She knew him better than most people. But more than that, she understood him. Not just who he was, but what he was. Who he had been, who he was always going to be. And that was something he never thought was possible. Some days, he wasn't sure he understood those things himself.

Their lives were a chaotic storm of madness. But whatever calm was in the center of that storm, it came from her. On that roof, with smoke and fire chasing at his heels, and Jessop fighting like an animal to destroy him, Shane realized that he needed that. He needed the calm. He needed to be grounded.

He needed her.

"Jacinta Perez, will you marry me?"

It was not a romantic proposal. Guys in movies did it in parks by fountains, or under the Eiffel Tower. But Shane didn't want to get wet with fountain spray, and he didn't need to visit France. The hallway in a hospital was as good as he needed it to be. He wasn't going to pretend to be someone else. And he didn't think he'd ever find someone like her.

He thought briefly that he should have bought a ring. People did that, too. And then it occurred to him that he didn't really need to.

Shane pulled his hand from his pocket. The iron ring in his palm was plain and utilitarian. It was not a beautiful or delicate thing, not the sort of shiny bauble that people associated with an engagement ring. But for him, for her, it meant something more. It was something that had kept him alive.

She looked at the ring sitting on his palm, and for a moment, Shane had the feeling that he had ruined it all. Instead, she covered her mouth with her hand for a moment, her eyes downcast at the ring, and she made a sound caught somewhere between a laugh and a sob.

"Oh Shane," she said quietly. She looked up, her eyes locking on his. "Of course I will."

She held her hand out, and he tried to place the ring on her finger. It was far too large, and she laughed as it slipped all the way to the base of her finger and dangled there. She removed it quickly, slipping it over her thumb, where it fit enough to not fall right off.

Her arms wrapped around him. Her embrace was tight, fervent, and he allowed himself a smile as he returned it.

Deep in his mind, part of him said this was a mistake. Not that Jacinta was a mistake, but this action. Because of who he was, and what he did. But if he lived by those rules, those fears, then what was he living for at all? Something had to change. He had been living the same way for too long.

Shane Ryan knew what misery was better than most. He knew all too well the depths of sorrow a person could hold; sorrow that could drag them back from beyond and fuel them for eternity. He knew the kind of fear and anger and loneliness that could infect a soul like a disease.

And he didn't want that. Not if someone like Jacinta wanted to be with him.

She kissed him, and he kissed her back. Doctors and patients wandered the halls, some eyeballing them with confusion or amusement. But it didn't matter what those people thought. None of them mattered.

They separated, and she raised her hand to look at the iron ring again.

"I can get you a better one if you like," Shane said. "A diamond ring?"

"No, this is perfect." She was still beaming from ear to ear. "But a resize couldn't hurt."

She kissed him again, pulling his hand to take him away from Dayton's room.

They had plans to make, and people to tell.

They had a life to start together.

If you enjoyed the book, please leave a review. Your reviews inspire us to continue writing about the world of spooky and untold horrors!

Check out these best-selling books from our talented authors

Ron Ripley (Ghost Stories)
- Berkley Street Series Books 1 – 9
  www.scarestreet.com/berkleyfullseries
- Moving in Series Box Set Books 1 – 6
  www.scarestreet.com/movinginboxfull

A. I. Nasser (Supernatural Suspense)
- Slaughter Series Books 1 – 3 Bonus Edition
  www.scarestreet.com/slaughterseries

David Longhorn (Sci-Fi Horror)
- Nightmare Series: Books 1 – 3
  www.scarestreet.com/nightmarebox
- Nightmare Series: Books 4 – 6
  www.scarestreet.com/nightmare4-6

Sara Clancy (Supernatural Suspense)
- Banshee Series Books 1 – 6
  www.scarestreet.com/banshee1-6

For a complete list of our new releases and best-selling horror books, visit www.scarestreet.com/books

See you in the shadows,
Team Scare Street